FOUR STEPS
TO DEATH

John Wilson

KCP FICTION

An Imprint of Kids Can Press

KCP Fiction is an imprint of Kids Can Press

Kids Can Press acknowledges the financial support of the Government of Ontario, through the Ontario Media Development Corporation's Ontario Book Initiative; the Ontario Arts Council; the Canada Council for the Arts; and the Government of Canada, through the BPIDP, for our publishing activity.

The author wishes to acknowledge a grant from the Project Assistance for Creative Writers program of the British Columbia Arts Council.

Published in Canada by
Kids Can Press Ltd.
29 Birch Avenue
Toronto, ON M4V 1E2

Published in the U.S. by
Kids Can Press Ltd.
2250 Military Road
Tonawanda, NY 14150

www.kidscanpress.com

Edited by Charis Wahl
Cover illustrations and interior maps by Céleste Gagnon
Interior designed by Céleste Gagnon and Kathleen Collett
Printed and bound in Canada

CM 05 0 9 8 7 6 5 4 3 2 1
CM PA 05 0 9 8 7 6 5 4 3 2 1

Library and Archives Canada Cataloguing in Publication

Wilson, John (John Alexander), 1951–
    Four steps to death / John Wilson.

ISBN 1-55337-704-4 (bound).   ISBN 1-55337-705-2 (pbk.)

1. Stalingrad, Battle of, Volgograd, Russia, 1942–1943 — Juvenile literature. I. Title.

PS8595.I5834F69 2005   jC813'.54   C2004-907186-6

Kids Can Press is a /©ⁿ∪S™ Entertainment company

*For Iain, in the hope that he will never
have a war to go to.*

PREFACE

More lives were lost in the battle for Stalingrad (over a million), than in most previous wars. It was also the turning point of the Second World War: before it, the German army appeared unstoppable; after it, the Germans never won a major battle. Russia's allies, the United States, Britain and Canada among them, were not directly involved in the battle; however, had the Russians lost, the Germans would have remained in control in the East, the war would have been much longer and costlier, and perhaps D-Day would not have been possible. We might live in a very different world today if Stalingrad had been the German victory that Hitler wanted. This is the story of a few soldiers, on both sides, who fought at Stalingrad.

DISCOVERY

Saturday, December 25, 2004

S E R G E I

It's winter in Volgograd and a gusting, knife-edged wind drives stinging ice crystals and small, hard snowflakes over the frozen Volga River. Around the building site, piles of earth and stacks of wood push blackly through the dirty snow like the sores of some leprous illness. Above, the heavy twilight sky threatens more snow.

Sergei Illyich Andropov draws his fur-lined parka tighter against the wind. He curses as he painfully bruises his shin on a protruding piece of angle iron.

What am I doing here? he asks himself. I'm too old for this kind of thing.

Sergei's bones ache. All he wants to do is sleep. By this time on a Saturday he should be on his way home, fighting other commuters on overcrowded buses instead of stumbling over this treacherous ground.

He laughs ruefully. It's Christmas Day most everywhere

except in Russia, where people still follow the old Julian calendar. Here Christmas is still thirteen days away. Not that Sergei's celebration would be that sumptuous. He has no money for luxuries, and home is a few square meters in a gray high-rise with a view across a narrow courtyard to an identical building. But at least it is somewhere he can keep warm for a few hours, and it is immeasurably better than when he was a kid during the war.

Sergei has lived all his life in this city. Born here seventy years ago, only ten years after the city changed its name from Tsaritsyn to Stalingrad, he has seen the great factories built, destroyed in the war and rebuilt. He has seen Stalingrad become Volgograd, after the mighty river that runs past it, and he has seen the Communists fall and capitalism take hold. Sergei shakes his head. The new capitalism — just another broken promise. At least the Communists looked after the old people — not well, but enough to keep them alive. Now they are on their own, not a profitable capitalist investment. That's why Sergei is still working long after he should have retired. Why he is tramping across a building site on this bleak afternoon after the foreman called to say that his men had discovered two bodies during excavation.

Another lousy gangland killing, Sergei thinks bitterly. There'll be a lot of paperwork and some fine-sounding platitudes about curbing organized crime; but nothing will be done and the crime will never be solved — too many people in high places are making too much money in bribes. It's all a charade.

Sergei spits disgustedly into the snow. Ahead, a portable arc light has been set up, its harsh glow forming a circle on the ground around which a few workmen stand, smoking. One notices Sergei's approach and comes to meet him.

"I'm the foreman, Yuri Andreavitch," the man says without preliminaries. "I hope this won't hold up work too long. We've got a tight schedule here and we're already behind. There'll be hell to pay if the foundations aren't in before the frost gets too hard."

Sergei nods listlessly. "Constable Andropov," he mumbles. He doesn't care about this man's problems. "Let's see the bodies."

"They're over here," Andreavitch says, leading the way. "The digger opened up some kind of basement. They're deep down and we didn't know if you'd get here before dark, so we set up the light. Not that it shows much. But there's two of them. Looks like they've been there for a while. Maybe it's a job for the archaeology boys, but we thought we'd better call the police first."

Thanks very much. Sergei grimaces. His leg, where a wall had fallen on him more than sixty years ago, is aching from the cold and strain. He rubs the muscle distractedly.

"Kind of old for police work, aren't you?" Andreavitch asks.

Sergei ignores him, and the ring of workers shuffles aside to let him through. At his feet is a large irregular hole. At the bottom, a black patch shows where the "basement room" is.

That'll be where the bodies are.

"Anybody have some light?" Sergei asks, hoping for a negative reply.

A large flashlight is passed forward. Sergei shines it experimentally into the hole. It has a good strong beam but doesn't show much — some broken wooden rafters, what might once have been a table and a booted foot. Sergei sighs. There is no other way — he will have to go down.

He works his way into the hole, concentrating on his footing as he balances the heavy torch. He's at the level of the basement before he can point the light at the reason he has had to drag out his old bones this afternoon. The grinning mummified face seems to leap forward in the dancing beam. Sergei recoils and the torch clatters to the ground at his feet.

"You okay?" a voice from above asks.

"Yeah!" Sergei answers angrily as he retrieves the light. He's annoyed at himself. How many bodies has he seen in his career with the police? Hundreds, and many in a much worse state than this. Yet here he is reacting like a rookie.

The hole is irregular and no more than three meters in any direction. The roof is the angled, collapsed concrete floor of what had been the level above. Two walls are relatively smooth and define the corner of what was a large basement room — either of a factory or an apartment complex. The other walls and floor are irregular masses of collapsed debris.

A musty smell hovering in the cold air tells Sergei that this space has been sealed for a very long time. That would account for the preservation of the bodies.

The corpse that shocked Sergei is sitting propped up against a smooth wall. Brown parchment skin is stretched over the skull, revealing startlingly white teeth in a hideous grin. The black, empty eye sockets seem to stare, as if angry that the body's long rest has been disturbed.

The corpse is dressed in rotted rags through which Sergei can glimpse white bone and withered brown tendon. A skeletal hand is draped over a rusted rifle. One leg is bent underneath the other, which sticks straight out and ends in the booted foot Sergei saw from above.

The second body lies on its side, legs crushed under a pile of bricks, hips oddly twisted. The corpse's face has been worked at by some small rodent, and only patches of skin remain attached to the pale skull. There is a neat, round bullet hole near the top.

This is no recent gangland crime. It's a much older drama.

"Well?" A voice intrudes from above. "Is this a police matter? Was there a murder here?"

Sergei pushes himself upright and squints into the light. "There were a million murders here."

"What'd you say?"

"Nothing. No, this isn't a police matter. Call the war graves people. They can take the bodies up to the memorial park on Mamaev Kurgan. Then you can get back to work."

"Great. I was afraid there'd be some long story here."

"Oh," Sergei says, "there's a story here, all right. Listen, I've got a couple of things I want to check out. I'm going to stay down here for a bit."

"Please yourself. I've got better things to do."

Footsteps move away and Sergei is left alone. Suddenly feeling very old and tired, he sits on a block of concrete and stares at the corpses. Half an hour ago, he was desperate to get home. Now he's sitting in a dark hole with two very old bodies, breathing air and dust that have been trapped for more than half a century.

Ancient stories, homeless and drifting, swirl around Sergei, clamoring to be heard. Almost-forgotten images fill his head. In a bewildering instant, Stuka dive-bombers scream, and Katyusha rockets wail in his ears. The smell of countless corpses assaults his nostrils, and the thunder of artillery shakes the ground so hard that he has to reach out to reassure himself that the pile of rubble he sits on is real.

Sergei sees his mother now, standing amid the city's ruins wearing an old greatcoat, her head wrapped in a thick woolen scarf. She is calling him away from some childish activity, "Sergei! Come here. You'll get into trouble." He smiles at the memory. He is eight years old, living in the midst of the greatest battle in human history. How can he get into any more trouble?

The shadows of the two bodies flicker and jump in Sergei's flashlight beam. The skulls grin at him.

"Who are you?" Sergei asks.

D A Y 1

T H E A D V E N T U R E B E G I N S

Friday, June 19, 1942

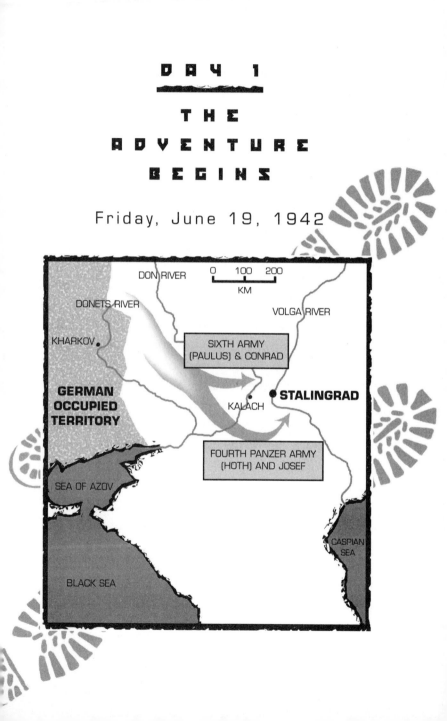

CONRAD

Conrad Zeitsler felt like a giant as he strolled through the ancient streets of Kharkov, seven hundred kilometers south of Moscow. He was almost a full head taller than his companion, but he held his back straight to squeeze every extra centimeter from his thin frame. In his freshly pressed black uniform with its silver insignia glinting in the spring sun, he looked like a large bird of prey. The impression was heightened by his long face, high, sharp cheekbones and hawklike nose. His pale blue eyes darted back and forth as if he was hunting.

Beside him, his older brother, Josef, was built more like the sturdy, squat tanks the pair commanded. His head was crowned with an unruly mop of red hair, a throwback to some long-ago Celtic heritage. The hair, small nose and sleepy brown eyes made it difficult to believe that the two shared the same parents, yet they did. Conrad had inherited his father's aristocratic bearing, which had stayed with the family generations after the estates in East Prussia had been sold off. Josef looked like their mother, a small, quick woman with an olive complexion more suited to a Mediterranean climate than the Black Forest, where she had grown up.

Kharkov had not been seriously damaged in the fighting the previous winter; walking between its stately buildings, the brothers could imagine that the war was a long way off. But the war was very close. Uniformed soldiers lounged everywhere, and rumbling columns of trucks and horse-drawn carts clogged the wide streets. The smell of frying sausage, gasoline and brick dust hung everywhere. An air of excited anticipation pervaded the occupying army — the great summer offensive that would end the war in the East was due to start in a few days, and despite the setbacks of the Russian winter offensives, expectations were high.

Germany's war to conquer Europe was almost three years old. Already Poland, France, Holland, Belgium, Scandinavia and most of European Russia had fallen to Hitler's armies led by the elite armored divisions. Conrad, at eighteen, was too young to have been part of those offensives — the coming attack would be his first battle — but Josef, four years older, was already a veteran.

"Being tall may have some advantages," Josef conceded, "but what about all those cuts and bruises you picked up in training? There's not much room in a Panzer Mark IV tank, and armor plating isn't goose down."

"I know that only too well," Conrad said. "But when I stand in my turret out on the flat steppe, I can see farther than you. I can spot a hidden gully or a camouflaged Russian antitank gun earlier."

"True. But if I want to be taller, I can stand on a block of wood. To be shorter, you'd have to take a saw to your ankles."

The pair laughed good-naturedly.

"A few bruises don't matter," Conrad went on. "We'll finish the Russians off this year. They can't have any reserves left after their losses last winter. We'll be on the Volga River by August. Then it will all be over. We'll control Europe, and Russia's allies will be helpless. America is busy with the Japanese in the Pacific, and Britain will make peace. Simple."

"Don't be so sure, little brother. Everyone said the Russians were finished last October, and look at the hard fighting there has been since then. The Volga is a long way off."

"But we are better equipped and better trained than the Ivans. Even if they have some reserves, we always beat them in open battle."

"I don't know. I can't shake this bad feeling when I look at the maps and see how far we are from home. We travel for weeks and don't seem to get anywhere."

"But we will get somewhere this year. Stalingrad — Stalin's own city on the Volga. Once we get there, we've won. Then we can go home."

"You're probably right." Josef pulled himself out of his mood and gave Conrad a friendly punch on the arm. "It *will* be over this year, and we'll be washing the dust off our clothes in the Volga long before winter.

"Look, I want to give you this." Josef held out a black-and-white ribbon, from which hung a silver-bordered black medal — the Iron Cross First Class. It had been awarded to Josef and Conrad's father in the Great War for "conspicuous bravery" in destroying a French machine-gun nest at Verdun in 1916. Yet it had come at a cost: their father had been shot in the chest, and the wound had become infected. He had survived, but throughout their childhood, their father had been unable even to climb a flight of stairs without gasping. While Conrad's friends played sports and went hiking with their fathers, Conrad spent much of his time at home tending to an invalid.

Conrad sometimes wondered what his life would have been like if his father hadn't been a hero and hadn't been wounded. When he was little, Conrad had loved to sneak into his parents' bedroom, take the medal out of its silk-lined case and gaze at the imperial crown, the oak leaf cluster and the date, 1914, embossed on the cold metal. He imagined his father the hero charging bravely against the machine-gun nest to save his comrades. But then he thought of all the things his father couldn't do. Sometimes he found himself wishing he could exchange the medal and all that heroism for a whole father.

The Iron Cross had fallen to Josef, as the older son, when their father had eventually succumbed to his wound in the spring of 1938. Josef, who worshiped his father, had carried the medal through the victories of his war.

"But Father left it to you," Conrad said.

"Yes, and I have treasured it. Often when we were in a tight spot these past three years, I'd take it out and think of Father's war. I've always been grateful that we can drive over open country in tanks and don't have to live like moles in dugouts and trenches. I think Father was a hero just to go through that war, never mind the machine-gun nest.

"Anyway, now I've seen and done a lot that Father could only imagine. You are starting out on this road, and I'm not so sure it will be as easy as you think. So take the medal. Keep it close and remember Father's bravery when you get in a fix."

"Thank you, Josef," Conrad said, accepting the medal, "but only as a loan. I will return it to you after this campaign is over."

"Fair enough." Josef smiled.

Conrad was honored that his brother was giving him something he held so precious, but the act also confused him. Shortly before his father had died, his mother was out working to supplement her husband's pension and Conrad had spent the day tending his bedridden father. As he finally settled the old man for what he hoped would be a quiet night, his father suddenly grabbed Conrad's arm. He had been very sick and his mind's hold on reality wavered much of the time, but now his eyes were bright.

"Promise me something. When I die — not long now — I want you to throw away that damned medal."

"Why?" Conrad had asked, bewildered.

"I should have tossed it years ago. Do you know what I see when I look at it?"

Conrad shook his head.

"I see the dead. I see the faces of the three machine gunners I killed." His gaze drifted across the darkened room to something far away — or long ago.

"Two were killed by the grenade I threw, but the third was only wounded. I could have taken him prisoner — he couldn't have done me any harm — but I didn't think of that. I jumped over the sandbags and plunged my bayonet into his chest. He just looked … surprised. I tried to pull the bayonet out, but it was jammed between his ribs. I pulled as hard as I could, braced my foot against his chest, but it wouldn't budge. He even tried to help, pushing on my rifle, but it was no use. We just sat and looked at each other.

"The only way to disengage a jammed bayonet is to fire the weapon. This is easy if you are shooting a corpse, but he couldn't have been much older than you are." The eyes flickered back to Conrad's face. "To shoot a man when he is alive and looking at you from an arm's length is a different matter.

"I fired, of course — there was no alternative — but that boy's face has never left me. And for that they gave me a medal!" He laughed ironically, and it quickly degenerated into a violent coughing fit. Then the old man went on. "Funniest thing was, I was shot on the way back to our lines. The doctors dug out a German bullet. It wasn't a French boy that nearly killed me, it was one of our own."

Conrad never told Josef what his father had said that night. When he came home for the funeral, all Josef could talk about was his training and how tanks were going to revolutionize warfare and make it again the noble adventure it had once been. Conrad didn't have the heart to shatter his brother's illusions when he saw how thrilled Josef was to receive the medal.

But now it was his.

"I'll look after it," Conrad said in a choked voice that he hoped Josef would take for overwhelming gratitude.

Josef nodded. "Good."

The strains of a piano, expertly played, drifted out of a nearby window.

"Listen," Josef said, waving his hand in the air in time to the music. "Brahms. Now there was a real composer. Much better than your Wagner, with all that doom and death."

"Brahms was a wimp," Conrad said with a laugh. "You can't beat Wagner opera for gods, heroes, battles — it's great."

"I admit Wagner's exciting," Josef said, "but I prefer something a little more peaceful."

He raised his hand to stop Conrad's response. "I guess we'll just have to disagree on music, but one thing is certain — we'll never win this war if we don't get back to our units."

The brothers embraced and parted, Josef to his battle-hardened crew in Hoth's Fourth Panzer Army and Conrad to his newly trained crew in the 16th Panzer Division of the XIV Panzer Corps.

"Race you to Stalingrad!" Conrad called after Josef. He was answered with a wave.

As Conrad made his way back to his tank, his father's words faded. His confidence, his sense of destiny, returned. His father had been only one in a long line of Zeitslers who had fought for their country. A great-uncle had helped defeat the French at Sedan in 1870. A Zeitsler had been an officer in Frederick the Great's army at the famous victory at Leuthen in 1757, and the family told of a Baron Manfred Zeitsler who had accompanied Frederick Barbarossa on the Third Crusade to the Holy Land in 1190. No wonder Conrad felt proud to belong to the spearhead of a new German army that was sweeping all its enemies before it. He felt lucky to live in such wonderful times.

Now, if only his chest would fill out his uniform, it would be a perfect world.

S E R G E I

Sergei is seven years old once more. He feels oddly disconnected, as if watching a movie he is starring in. The past is as real as the present: he is an old man sitting beneath a building site in 2004 and a boy playing in the vacant lot behind his apartment block in the center of Stalingrad in the summer of 1942.

The boys from the apartment block are playing their endless game of Communists versus Fascists. As always, Sergei has been cast as a Fascist. Only the older boys and those in the Young Communist League get to be Communists. They always win. Sergei doesn't want to die again.

"Bang! You're dead!"

"Am not!" Sergei yells, swerving violently to his right. A low fence catches his foot and flings him headlong into the soft earth of Tolstoy's turnip allotment. Dirt and young turnip plants fly in all directions. The warm smell of soft earth assails Sergei's nostrils.

"You're in for it now," the boy who had shot Sergei says in awe.

Being caught by Tolstoy is immeasurably worse than being shot as a Fascist. The old man is slow but unforgiving, and his slap can leave your ears ringing for hours.

Panic stricken, Sergei scrambles to his feet and frantically tries to brush the telltale dirt off his trousers.

"Hey!"

An old man with a shock of white hair and a weather-beaten face is waving a rough stick at him from the far side of the allotment. Tolstoy. Sergei's heart sinks. The old man never forgets, and one day when Sergei is least expecting it, a gnarled hand will reach out from the shadows of a hallway.

Sergei leaps the fence and sprints across the vacant lot.

"I've seen you, Sergei Illyich Andropov. Don't think I haven't."

Sergei's mother appears at a second-floor window of the apartment block. "Sergei. Are you getting into trouble again?"

He is never out of trouble.

Where had that memory come from? Conjuring up old Tolstoy and that childish game out of thin air? In some strange way, Sergei feels he has momentarily brought them all back to life — his mother, the famous sniper who had been his hero and the countless dead soldiers — even the one he killed.

VASILY

Vasily Sarayev cradled his precious PPSH41 sub-machine gun to his chest. The weapon still smelled oily and left spots of factory grease on his uniform, but the important thing was that his new gun, set to full fire, could spray hundreds of bullets a minute. Vasily was going to kill dozens of the Fascist invaders.

After only three weeks' training at the barracks in Moscow, he had been made a platoon scout in the famous 13th Guards Rifle Division. The training had been rudimentary and as much of it political as military — some trainees still didn't know how their rifles worked — but Vasily had been conscientious. He had concentrated, worked hard and shown an aptitude for the mechanical side of things. Among the new recruits, he held the record for stripping and reassembling a machine gun blindfolded — forty-two seconds. That was why he had been made a scout.

After his training, Vasily had been given twenty-four hours' leave but now he had to report to the 13th Guards' transit camp south of Moscow. It would be his first time outside the city — and his first train journey. He was nervous, but proud. Last fall, he had helped dig antitank ditches when Fascist tanks threatened Moscow's suburbs. Over the winter, the Germans had been driven back; but there was talk of a new attack to come, in the south. This time, Vasily would do more than dig ditches. He and his machine gun would throw the invaders back to Berlin where they belonged. It was a wonderful time.

Vasily stood on platform five of the Moscow railway station, surrounded by a surging mass of soldiers jostling to get a seat in the line of carriages that lay waiting amid the clouds of steam drifting back from the engine. A cacophony of voices, shouting commands, yelling instructions and calling farewells, echoed through the cavernous building.

Many of the soldiers were seventeen, like Vasily, but he looked much younger. He was of average height, slightly built and had inherited his mother's round face and large brown eyes, which had always made him look boyish. He had been teased at school and at the factories where he had apprenticed as a machinist. Often it had been good-humored, but occasionally there had been a cruel edge — "mama's boy" and "baby" had hurt. Vasily had learned to take the insults quietly — that was less painful than the fights that followed his objection, but now it was all over. Here he was, a soldier going off to fight for his country. No one would dare call him a mama's boy now.

Ironically, Vasily could barely remember his mother. She had died in a factory accident when he was four. Since then he had been brought up by his father, an old-guard Communist who had fought to get rid of the czar in 1917.

"Our country is showing the world how to live," he used to say. "It is hard, but it is also a great responsibility. You are too young to remember how it was before 1917, but every one of us must help the revolution succeed."

When Vasily was little his father's comrades from the revolution and the civil war had come round. They would drink vodka and stand around the chipped and scratched piano that dominated their tiny living room, singing rousing revolutionary songs and keeping time by slapping their thighs and stamping their feet. Vasily could recall tottering among the legs of the singers. Sometimes, huge hands would descend, as if from the heavens, and lift him abruptly into the air. Grinning, hairy faces would loom in and out as he was passed around and tossed toward the ceiling. He would laugh and gurgle until his tiny sides ached.

The evenings always ended with storytelling. Vasily would curl up on the floor wrapped in his blanket and listen to the tales the old men told — about talking animals, witches and brave princes on dangerous quests. His favorites were about a peasant farmer scratching out a living at the edge of a dark, magical forest. The man had countless adventures with the animals of the forest and always managed to outsmart them. Try as he might to stay awake, Vasily's eyes always closed with stories still swirling around him.

As the years passed, the visitors became fewer as the old comrades aged and died, but Vasily's father continued to love music and taught his son to play the piano. Vasily could still beat out any number of popular songs, but he had never taken to the boring classical pieces his father had tried to teach him. He preferred a good tune with rousing words that could be belted out at a party. No one could sing along to Shostakovitch.

When the Fascists invaded in June 1941, Vasily's father had encouraged him to join the army. "It is unpatriotic to put personal wants and desires ahead of the struggle to free Russia from the invader. Comrade Stalin is leading the way to a bright new future where no one will be exploited at the hands of corrupt royalists and greedy businessmen. We cannot let the Fascists destroy that. An individual's life is nothing compared to freedom."

It was a message that Vasily heard everywhere, from his father, on the radio, from his teachers, and it inspired him — he was going to make his father proud. Earlier Vasily had been turned down as too young for military service, but so many soldiers had been killed or captured that his youth was no longer a handicap.

He smiled as he remembered the obvious pride in his father's eyes when he had told him he had been accepted for the army.

"I am glad to see you smiling!" Vasily's father shouted above the roar of hissing steam, clanging carriage doors and shouted orders. "These are extraordinary times and we must prove ourselves worthy of them."

"I will be," Vasily replied. "I will kill Fascists for you."

"Good. Communism must survive, our revolution must remain secure. Our will shall triumph. Whatever happens, Vasily, you must remember that."

"Yes, Father." But he was having trouble concentrating on his father's inspiring words. The great hissing train on which he would soon be racing through the countryside was drawing his attention.

His father embraced him once and pushed him toward the nearest carriage. Vasily fought his way to the door through the crush of soldiers. He had no chance of finding a seat, so he dumped his pack on the floor of the corridor, staking out a space.

Still holding his machine gun, he leaned out the window as the last carriage doors slammed and the train jerked awkwardly forward. Vasily's heart leaped. A sea of shouting faces moved past as the train gathered speed. Some women, many crying as they ran, tried to keep pace with the train, but they were soon left behind. Vasily leaned out and glanced along the platform. His father stood immobile, a hand raised in farewell.

The train exploded out of the station in a cloud of smoke and noise. Buildings flashed by, and Vasily had the unsettling feeling that the world was rushing backward beneath him.

Eventually he fought his way to his pack and sat on the floor. Some soldiers had brought food, and the strong smell of sausage wafted through the carriages. An older man with the weather-beaten face of a peasant sat beside Vasily.

"How old are you, son?" he asked in a rough, country accent.

"I'm seventeen, Comrade," Vasily replied defensively.

"So, they are sending out pups. Uncle Joe must be getting desperate."

Vasily had never heard Joseph Stalin, the great leader whose face stared down from countless huge posters on every street corner, talked about in such familiar or rude terms.

"Don't look so startled," the old soldier went on. "In the army you get bad food, lousy beds and plenty of opportunities to die for your country. The one advantage is that you can speak your mind among your comrades. What's your unit?"

"Rodimtsev's 13th Guards Rifle Division," Vasily said proudly. "I am a scout."

"My division," the old man said. "Rodimtsev's a good man."

"I have heard," Vasily said eagerly, "that his men would choose death over being transferred to another unit."

The old soldier laughed roughly. "Maybe so, but I've never met one. In my experience, the only things worth dying for are a good pair of boots and a bottle of vodka. The name's Yevgeny."

"Vasily." The pair shook hands.

"Rodimtsev's not like some of the drunken butchers I've seen," Yevgeny went on. "You're lucky there, but get out of scouting as soon as you can. The scout is always the first man of a squad killed in an attack."

"It is an honor to die for Russia," Vasily said, to cover his shock.

"Of course it is. But I would like to put it off as long as possible."

Vasily hoped there weren't too many such cynics in the army. Not that it mattered —Vasily was going to be a hero. He imagined himself on one of the posters that seemed to cover every empty wall in Moscow — jaw set, red flag held high, head wound bandaged, urging his men forward with a dramatic wave of his pistol. Now Vasily was just a lowly rifleman, but he was sure he would get his chance to become a hero like Rodimtsev.

As Vasily daydreamed, the train rattled through the wasteland of smoke-blackened factories on Moscow's outskirts, past the trenches and tank ditches that had stopped the German offensive last year and into the countryside. His adventure was beginning.

DAY 30

EARLY VICTORIES

Saturday, July 18, 1942

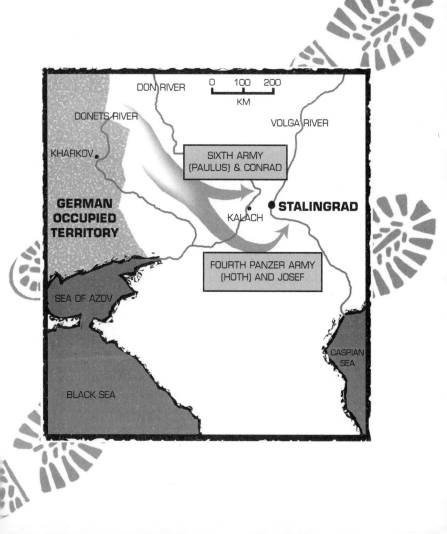

CONRAD

Conrad was at sea on an ocean of yellow and green. All around him, fields of waving sunflowers and ripening stalks of corn stretched to the horizon, the view broken only by desolate columns of black smoke from burning farms. Above him, the sun hung, hazy through the dust thrown up by the line of tanks. The attack was going splendidly: they had broken through the Russian defenses and were in open country.

Conrad adjusted his goggles and squinted. A motorcycle dispatch-rider was working his way back along the column. Conrad glanced back. The dozen soldiers in the open half-track behind, happy not to be walking, waved cheerfully at him. Conrad raised his arm in response. He was glad too — glad he was in the open air and not below in the noisy, cramped belly of the tank. Conrad only breathed dust; below, it stank overpoweringly of gasoline, grease and stale bodies. But all five of the crew loved Lili, as they had named their tank, after their favorite song, "Lili Marlene." Lili was their home. They traveled in her, fought from her, ate beside her and slept beneath her.

Lili's crew was Conrad's new family — Franz, the driver, undoubtedly cursing colorfully at the blinding dust, although Conrad could hear nothing over the heavy rumble of the tank's motor; Gottfried, the outspoken gunner who, despite his thick glasses, could hit the silhouette of a Russian T-34 tank at fifteen hundred meters; Heinz, the radio operator, even younger than Conrad and always bragging about his many girlfriends back in Munich; and Erich, the loader, a farmer who gazed in envious awe at the vast fields they stopped in every night.

They were a family, but Conrad was its head. At first there had been some skepticism about his ability to lead because of his age. Erich, the oldest of the crew, had made sly gibes about what high-ranking Nazi Conrad might know to swing the commander's job at eighteen. That had just been during training; now that they were at war, Erich had fallen silent as they learned to work together, and Conrad's competence and cheerfulness won them over.

The throaty roar of the dispatch-rider drawing level distracted Conrad. He watched as the messenger maneuvered along the edge of the congested road. Lucky man — after delivering his message to head-quarters, he would be able to relax in safety for a little, maybe even have a wash. Apart from splashing cold water on his face, Conrad hadn't washed in days. He dreamed of soaking in a deep tub of hot water.

Odd popping sounds reached Conrad over the noise of Lili's engine. Puzzled, he glanced over his shoulder just as the explosion erupted behind him and the dispatch-rider's limp body cartwheeled into the ditch. His motorcycle followed in a graceful arc before crashing to the ground. The half-track was slewed crazily to one side, its front end on fire and both men in the cab dead. The other soldiers were scrambling out of the back, weapons at the ready.

Already Franz had brought Lili to a halt, and Gottfried was preparing to rotate the turret. Conrad scanned the fields. There! Dark patches amid the green corn. Conrad grabbed his binoculars and focused: five Russian soldiers were clustered around a handheld antitank rocket launcher. Two were reloading, and three were firing small arms at the column. The soldiers from the half-track were returning fire. As Conrad watched, one of the Russians crumpled to the ground.

Conrad leaned down into the turret. "Swivel left 110 degrees. One round and machine-gun fire at Ivans with a launcher in the cornfield."

With a mechanical rumble, the turret began to rotate. Conrad could hear Erich ramming a shell into the breach and Heinz cocking the machine gun. As the turret moved, Conrad turned his attention back to the Russians. They had almost reloaded and were aiming the launcher at Lili. They had been aiming at Lili when they hit the half-track, Conrad realized, and she was a sitting duck now.

The turret seemed to be moving painfully slowly. The machine gun, on its ball-joint mounting, would come to bear first, but even it was not in place yet. Conrad knew he should get into the turret, but he was mesmerized and didn't want to distract his crew, who were concentrating on saving Lili. Besides, if the Russian rocket hit Lili's thin side armor, in or out of the tank, they were all dead.

"Come on! Come on!" Conrad found himself muttering encouragingly. With a heavy, pounding clatter, the machine gun opened fire. Conrad could see the traversing bullets cutting down the corn to the Russians' left. One man, away from his comrades, was caught in the stomach and doubled over, but the others kept working. Conrad willed the turret to turn faster.

Heavy machine-gun bullets caught the three remaining Russians in a tight group and flung them backward. Either it caught them at the instant of firing or the operator's death grip triggered the launcher; in any case, the rocket shot wildly up in the air and exploded harmlessly in the field.

Conrad felt someone tug on his trouser leg. "Do you still want to put a shell into them?" Gottfried asked.

"No need," Conrad replied. Already the soldiers from the half-track were fanning out cautiously into the field to mop up and make sure there were no more unpleasant surprises. "Just keep the gun trained until we're sure it's all clear."

Conrad could feel his body relax as the adrenaline dissipated. "Good work, Heinz!" he shouted down the hatch. "You got them just in time."

"Easy," came back the cheerful, confident voice. "They didn't stand a chance."

Heinz was right, Conrad reflected. None of their enemies, none of Germany's enemies, stood a chance. This was their destiny, and the ghosts of Barbarossa, Frederick the Great and Bismarck were with them, willing them on to complete their task.

Conrad looked forward. The dust had settled, and he could clearly see the long line of tanks strung out across the steppe. Many tank crews had emerged for a breath of fresh air. Why weren't they moving?

At the front of the column, Hauptman Bernhard von Schmidt would be carefully assessing the situation. Rumor had it that the aristocratic von Schmidt had been disowned in disgrace after some scandal. With the perverse logic of soldiers, he was known affectionately as "the Baron" among the tank crews. Much of their affection was due to von Schmidt's caution. He was not indecisive but carefully weighed all options before ordering his men to risk their lives.

"Looks like we're stuck here for a while," Conrad shouted down. "Might as well have a smoke."

Almost immediately, the hatch in the side of the turret opened and Gottfried emerged. He was thin and studious, an effect heightened by the wire-rimmed glasses balanced on the bridge of his nose. He seemed to have read every book ever written, including those not approved by the government. Life was a serious business for Gottfried, but the others put up with his lack of humor because he was a fund of knowledge. As he peered around nervously from the hatch, he looked like a startled owl leaving its nest.

No one appeared less like a soldier or more like a bookworm than Gottfried. With his thick glasses, he didn't look as if he could see more than a few meters; yet he was the best shot in the battalion, something they all took much pride in, not least because it might save their lives one day.

With a cursory nod to Conrad, Gottfried dangled his long legs over the rear of the tank and lit a cigarette. "At last, a breath of air that doesn't smell of gasoline and Franz's socks."

Heinz's blond hair and babyish face followed Gottfried through the hatch, his perpetual smile firmly in place. Heinz was the crew's optimist, always ready with a joke or a story about one of his many girlfriends. His boyish good looks and wavy blond hair made him a virtual poster boy of the ideal Aryan. Sometimes he annoyed the others when he went on about how wonderful Hitler was and how many important things he had done for Germany, but only Gottfried argued with any passion. The others just smiled at his youthful enthusiasm.

"I envy you, Conrad," Heinz said, "sitting up here watching all the pretty farm girls."

"I haven't seen any today," Conrad responded. "I think their mothers must be keeping them indoors because they heard you were coming."

"You just want them all for yourself. But it won't work. You can't keep me cooped up in there forever, and you won't stand a chance once they see me."

Conrad smiled at Heinz's infectious good humor as the boy stretched luxuriously.

Erich emerged only halfway and sat on the lip of the hatch. "Franz wants to stay inside and fiddle with some valve that bothers him."

Franz was the only crew member who seemed completely content in the hot, cramped confines of the tank. It was a standing joke that he had missed his vocation and should have joined the U-boat service. Franz was gruff and swore more colorfully than the rest of them put together, but he had an almost obsessive concern with every little detail of Lili's mechanical health, making her one of the most reliable machines in the battalion. They all knew that Lili's reliability, like Gottfried's gunnery, could save their lives and, despite their teasing, were happy to leave Franz to his tinkering.

Erich scanned the fields around them with a practiced eye. He had a farmer's weather-beaten face, acquired during years of working the land in his native Thuringia. The deep lines around his eyes and the gray on his temples made him look even older than his years. They also made his eyes seem dramatic. They were a striking blue that contrasted with the old leather of his skin. Mostly they regarded the world with weary contempt from beneath hooded lids, but when there was land to be examined, they sparkled.

Erich seemed happy only when running soil through his fingers and pronouncing on what crops would grow well where. Conrad had thought it strange that a farmer should volunteer to be cooped up in a tank, but Erich had been told that there would be plenty of good farmland available after the conquest of Russia, and tank crews would get first pick.

Unlike Heinz and Gottfried, Erich cared nothing for politics. He had only one sensitive spot, his surname, Himmler, the same as that of the Nazi in command of the SS. Early on, Gottfried had made the mistake of teasing Erich about his name and they had almost come to blows. Since then, Gottfried had confined his teasing to Heinz, who accepted it good-naturedly.

"Good land, this," Erich said to no one in particular. "Needs irrigation, but it will have a fine crop of corn this year." Having pronounced on the suitability of this particular Russian field, Erich lapsed back into his customary silence.

Conrad's gaze was caught by a small dust cloud that eventually resolved itself into a second motorcycle. The rider came to a halt beside Lili, raised his goggles and wiped the sweat and dust from his face with his sleeve. "What happened?"

"Same old story," Conrad replied. "Five Ivans and a rocket launcher hid until we were almost past, then tried to take us in the rear. They were aiming for the tank, but got the courier and the half-track."

The soldier nodded. "I'll report to the Baron. With luck he'll send me back to headquarters, and I'll get a decent meal and a bath."

The soldier strode over to the messenger's body, removed a square leather pouch and tucked it into his waistband.

"What's holding us up?" Conrad asked.

"Oh, some Ivans up ahead. They've got a T-34 tank set up in a ruined farmhouse. But we spotted them before we got in range. The Baron's called for Stukas to sort them out. Here they come now."

Conrad shielded his eyes and looked up. A line of black shapes, like a flock of migrating geese, droned overhead.

Every eye in the column was gazing up at the sky now, grateful to the Stuka pilots thousands of meters above. They were an armored column's artillery and had, on countless occasions, destroyed troublesome defensive positions and broken up concentrations of Russian tanks.

By all accounts their commander, Baron Wolfram von Richthofen, a cousin of the famous Red Baron of Conrad's father's war, was a hard man. He was undoubtedly intelligent but also arrogant, and his brutality in sending his air armada against undefended cities had earned him a deserved reputation for ruthlessness.

"Just as well he's on our side," Erich had said, and Conrad had to agree. Whatever Richthofen's shortcomings, without his Stukas, the tanks would have a much harder time of it.

As Conrad watched, the lead plane peeled off. Although it was several kilometers away, Conrad could hear the wail of its siren. He was glad the "shrieking vulture" wasn't directly above *him*. It screamed down into a dive, followed by the others and, just when it seemed too late, pulled up to regain altitude.

Conrad couldn't see the bombs fall, but he heard the dull *crump* as they exploded and saw the column of smoke rise.

"Well, looks like they are doing their job," the motorcyclist said. "So I'd better get on with mine." Kicking his machine to life, he disappeared in a cloud of dust.

"Okay," Conrad said. "They've cleared our way. We'd better get Lili ready to go."

Conrad watched with pride as his crew returned to their duties like parts of a well-oiled machine. Life was perfect. Instinctively, he patted the hard metal of his twenty-ton tank. His Lili — her 30 mm of armor plating protected him and her 75 mm cannon and two heavy machine guns destroyed his enemies. With Lili, he could conquer the world. He reached into the left breast pocket of his black uniform and pulled out his father's medal. The metal was cold against his palm.

I wish you had lived to see this war, Father, he said to himself. It's glorious — a crusade against the barbarians.

Conrad pictured himself as a Teutonic knight of the Middle Ages, riding forth to do battle with the Russian hordes, as Wagner's magnificent music swelled in the background. But Conrad's steed was made of steel and came from one of Krupp's huge armaments factories in Essen.

Smiling, Conrad placed the medal back in his pocket.

"Let's go!" he yelled through the hatch as the column lurched forward. "It's a long way to the Volga."

SERGEI

"Bang, you're dead." Another Fascist falls to the ground.

It is Sergei's eighth birthday, and in honor of the occasion, he is allowed to be a Communist on the winning side. Even better, this morning, Pavel, the apartment block bully, was caught and soundly cuffed about the ears by Tolstoy for some long-ago misdemeanor — right out in the open where everyone could watch from a safe distance.

As soon as all the Fascists are taken care of, Sergei will head home to stuff his belly with his mother's delicious pork-and-turnip stew. After that, there will be fruit pie, hot from the oven. On top, his mother will have carved the traditional "S dniom razhdjenia, Sergei" — Happy Birthday, Sergei.

He salivates as he imagines the first bite — red rhubarb juice and chunks of fruit as the sour-sweet smell assaults his nostrils.

"Hey! Pay attention!" A boy is shouting at Sergei. He is the oldest and is always cast as Comrade Stalin. "How are we going to defeat the Fascists if all you can do is stand around dreaming. Get moving."

Galvanized into action, Sergei breaks into a crouching run. He aims his stick gun at a glimpse of back.

"Bang, you're dead."

"Am not!" The figure disappears around a corner. Sergei follows, legs pounding.

This is the best day of his life.

VASILY

The rhythmical clack of the rails beneath the train wheels was playing a tune in Vasily's head. He amused himself making up words to the staccato beat: we're going to the war. We're going to the war. It's going to be fun. It's going to be fun. We'll kill the invaders. We'll kill the invaders. And then we'll go home. And then we'll go home. It was almost as good as having his father's old piano to mess around on.

Vasily felt like singing out loud. Here he was, the scout for Squad 2, in B Platoon of H Company of the 52nd Rifle Battalion, 13th Guards Rifle Division. This second train journey of Vasily's life was in a cattle car, not a carriage, but it was equally crowded. All four squads from B Platoon were crammed into one car for their journey from the transit camp, south across the steppe to their division, congregated outside the city of Kamyshin. The Germans were attacking in the south this summer, and the Guards must be ready to rush to wherever the threat seemed most serious.

Vasily was lucky to have a spot close to the open door. From where he sat, he could get some fresh air and watch the endless flat landscape racing by outside. He would have preferred to sit on the edge and dangle his feet over the side, but at least he wasn't one of the men crammed in the dark rear of the wagon around the single stinking bucket that they all had to use.

If Vasily looked to his left, he could see the squad commander, Nikolai, sitting on a box and compulsively flicking a lighter made from an old cartridge case. Around him, the heavy machine gunner and his loader were trying to snatch some sleep. Yevgeny, the cynical old soldier from the Moscow train, sat nearby, surrounded by the four other riflemen in the squad. Vasily barely recognized these men, rough peasants from beyond the Urals who spoke in thick accents that he could hardly understand. The only person missing from the squad was a sniper, who was yet to be assigned.

These men, Yevgeny was fond of telling Vasily, were his family now — more than family. "Your mother gave you life. Your father gave you knowledge. Comrade Stalin gave you bread. But only the men of your squad will be with you when you die."

It was not very comforting, but Vasily was glad to be on his way south. The Germans had been advancing for weeks and he was impatient. How was he going to become a hero if he never met the enemy? He knew new recruits needed training, but so much of his time outside Moscow had been spent in pointless drills and listening to long political speeches that he was sometimes close to despair. The political instructors sounded just like his father. "Comrade Stalin knows that it is the will to win that distinguishes Russian soldiers from their German counterparts. They fight only for land and are far from home; we fight for an ideal with our backs to our own hearth. That is why we will win." Vasily believed them, but some practice in tactics and weapons training would be nice, too.

As far back as he could remember, Vasily had been told what he must do. His father, Comrade Stalin, everyone he talked to was absolutely certain that Russia was evolving exactly as it should toward an earthly paradise of equality and reason. No one questioned, no one needed to doubt. Just let the leaders do their jobs and all would be well. It was comforting. Vasily had known there were dissidents — the radio and newspapers talked about them being rooted out and reeducated — but they were aberrations, people with old ideas who couldn't adjust. Perhaps cynical Yevgeny was one of them? But then Vasily had questions too. Why didn't their training make sense? And why didn't anyone else seem to worry about it? Was he becoming a dissident? It was so confusing.

Vasily was roused from his thoughts by urgent voices. The men sitting in the doorway were gesturing at the sky and yelling something he couldn't make out over the rumble of the train wheels. He strained to see what they were pointing at. He could see nothing except the washed-out blue sky, but the rhythm of the wheels was slowing and a high-pitched whine was coming from the brakes.

Suddenly, the whine rose to a scream, and Vasily was thrown violently forward. The carriage lurched, hesitated for a moment and plunged off the tracks, throwing men and equipment in every direction. He saw a line of black dots, like angry seagulls, against the blue summer sky, before the walls of the carriage disintegrated and he was thrown into space. For an instant he was flying through the air — then he hit the ground and everything went black.

When Vasily opened his eyes, he was lying on his back, with his head propped against something soft. In front of him, the train lay alongside the track, split open like a fish on the slabs in the Moscow market. Carriages lay at all angles, some piled on top of others, some on their roofs. A few near the engine were on fire, belching scarlet flames, black smoke and horrible screams. The engine appeared to have exploded, and long curved pipes stuck out of its body like intestines, bleeding steam into the air. The ground around Vasily was littered with men, lying or sitting. Some were injured, some just looked stunned and some were lying on their backs, pointing rifles or machine guns into the air.

At first Vasily thought it was a simple train wreck, but then some of the shrieks resolved into a noise that was not human. The soldiers lying on their backs opened fire. Vasily tilted his head back and looked up.

A black shape was plummeting toward him — a bird, with V-shaped wings and talons reaching out to rip his body open. It was wailing with anticipation.

Vasily was paralyzed with fear. Around him, men were shooting wildly at the bird, to no effect. Then the bird leveled off. Vasily could see the pale gray underbelly and the hated black crosses on the wings. It wasn't a bird, it was a Stuka dive-bomber. As Vasily watched, a black dot wobbled away from the plane and fell toward him. One thing his training had taught him: that would be a 900 kg bomb.

The hot blast from the explosion washed over Vasily — sirens and men screamed, bombs exploded, machine guns chattered. When would it end?

Slowly Vasily realized that the back of his head felt wet. Was he wounded? He wasn't in pain. He thrust his hand behind him into warm softness. Blood. Puzzled, he rolled over. His head had been resting on what was left of the stomach of a rifleman from his squad. Vasily jackknifed forward and retched noisily. He couldn't even remember the dead man's name.

By the time his stomach was empty, the raid was over. Officers worked their way along the tracks organizing the stunned men into units. Vasily stumbled over to Nikolai, who was standing with several others of his squad.

Gradually the squads and then the platoon re-formed. Almost everyone was bruised or cut but, remarkably, they were mostly minor wounds. A man in another squad had a nasty gash in his forehead and someone else held his left arm across his chest, but the man beside Vasily was the only death in his platoon. Casualties had been much worse near the front of the train, where a row of charred corpses lay on the grass beside the burned-out cars.

"We were lucky," Nikolai observed.

"Lucky!" Yevgeny countered. "The Fascists were luckier. Where the hell's our air force?"

"They can't be everywhere," Vasily said.

"True," said Yevgeny, "and I'm sure Comrade Stalin has them performing worthwhile duties elsewhere, but it would be nice to see them occasionally. I don't like walking, and it looks as if we have a long hike in front of us."

The survivors collected what equipment they could salvage, formed up and began marching down the railway line. No mere raid could stop them. They would march until they got to Kamyshin or until another train picked them up. Vasily's spirits rose — that was the revolutionary spirit his father had talked of. Behind Vasily, someone began to sing. Soon everyone in the ragged column was singing at the top of his voice.

"Zemlyanka" was considered unpatriotic because of its pessimism, but there was no way to stop every soldier in the Red Army singing it. Vasily felt guilty singing a song not approved by the Party, but "Zemlyanka" was very beautiful and it always made him think of home.

The fire is flickering in the narrow stove
Resin oozes from the log like a tear
And the concertina in the bunker
Sings to me of your smile and eyes.

The bushes whispered to me about you
In a snow-white field near Moscow
I want you above all to hear
How sad my living voice is.

You are now very far away
Expanses of snow lie between us
It is so hard for me to come to you,
And here there are four steps to death.

Vasily felt tears sting his eyes.

"Thinking of a sweetheart back home?" Yevgeny asked.

"No," Vasily replied. "I don't have a girlfriend."

"Don't worry. Comrade Stalin has promised that we shall drive the invaders all the way back to Berlin. There will be lots of nice German girls for you to choose from when we get there."

Vasily blushed furiously. He knew more about his machine gun than he did about women, and he was less afraid of death than of a conversation with a pretty girl. With no sisters and only his father's rough friends for company, Vasily had never become comfortable in female presence. Not that he didn't want a girlfriend —

he ached for one and envied the boys at school who boasted of their conquests. It was just that as soon as a girl smiled at him, Vasily's mind froze. Even the simplest conversation deserted him and he stood helplessly slack-jawed and idiotic.

Once, some boys at school had told him that Marika, the class beauty, wanted to talk to him behind the school wall. It had taken Vasily several minutes and all his courage to force one foot in front of the other to the wall and around the corner.

Marika had been there, all right, but not alone. Alexei, the class commissar and leader of the local Young Communist League was wrapped around her. Both turned to look at the intruder. Marika wore an arrogant smile that still melted Vasily's knees in recollection.

"What do you want, mama's boy?" Alexei sneered.

Ears ringing with the laughter of his classmates, Vasily fled. For days afterward, he had to force himself to go to school to endure the snickers and cruel asides. After that he had studiously avoided any situation that might lead to contact with girls.

"Don't get too excited," Yevgeny added. "We have a lot of work to do before we get to Berlin."

DAY 66

ON THE VOLGA

Sunday, August 23, 1942

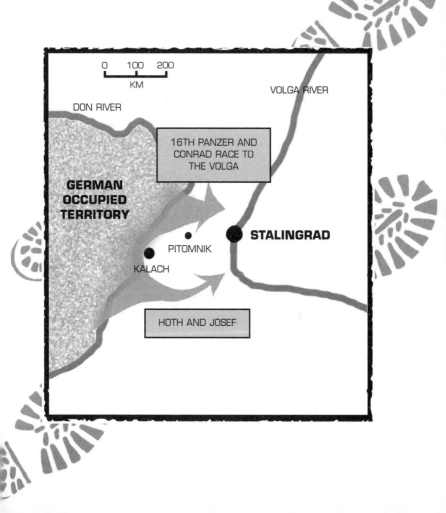

0   100   200
KM

VOLGA RIVER

DON RIVER

16TH PANZER AND
CONRAD RACE TO
THE VOLGA

**GERMAN
OCCUPIED
TERRITORY**

STALINGRAD

PITOMNIK

KALACH

HOTH AND JOSEF

CONRAD

Conrad sat with his back against Lili's tracks. Around him in the cherry orchard, the silhouettes of tanks, black against the predawn gray, the clang of mess tins and the scattered red glow of cigarettes told him the 16th Panzer Division was almost ready to get on with its day. Franz, Gottfried and Heinz still dozed beneath Lili's metal belly. Erich, with his almost supernatural ability to sniff out the last half-wild abandoned chicken or carefully hidden ham in a burned-out farm, was already off looking for breakfast.

The race across the steppe had been exhausting. The retreating Russian army had driven the livestock with them, leaving behind poisoned wells and burned farms — and partisans who appeared from nowhere to attack without warning. At night, planes dropped small annoying bombs that did little damage but disrupted sleep. By day, swarms of huge black flies — Stalin's secret weapon, the soldiers called them — seethed in masses on exposed food, making it impossible to eat or drink without swallowing a mouthful of the disgusting insects. More serious, dysentery and typhus were on the rise.

On the plus side, the Don Cossacks who inhabited the quaint whitewashed, thatched villages they passed through hated Stalin. The old men told about fighting against the Red Army in the great civil war of 1918 to 1920, of brutally supressed rebellions and deliberate starvation. Conrad liked the Cossacks and felt proud to be liberating such fiercely independent warriors.

Conrad was happy: today they would reach the Volga, the boundary between Europe and Asia and their goal. They would take Stalingrad and establish comfortable quarters before winter set in. Perhaps there would even be leave. With luck, Conrad and Josef might celebrate Christmas at home with their mother.

"What do you have to smile about?" Erich appeared out of the semidarkness. He held a lumpy handkerchief tied in a bundle.

"Eggs?" Conrad asked, ignoring the question.

"Right. But if those lazy good-for-nothings don't shift themselves soon we won't have time to eat before we move out."

"I'll wake them. You get the fire going." Conrad stood and kicked the feet sticking out from beneath the tank. "Come on, rise and shine. It's going to be another beautiful sunny day on the Eastern Front, and we have eggs for breakfast."

Slowly three figures emerged, grumbling, scratching and stretching. Franz had a disgusting brown, homemade cigarette between his lips. Smoking in the tank was forbidden, so Franz smoked only when they stopped, but the thin, drooping remains always hung from his lip, gradually absorbing saliva and turning an ever-increasingly revolting shade of brown.

"Did you sleep with that thing in your mouth?" Heinz asked brightly. "No wonder you can't get a girl."

The only reply was a grunt as Franz struck a match and struggled to relight the soggy stump.

Gottfried blinked shortsightedly in the poor light and wandered over to help Erich with the fire.

In only a few moments, a small blaze was swelling into life, and scrambled eggs, fried onions and black sausage were sizzling in the pan.

"The Volga today, boys, eh?" Heinz said, serving up the food and pouring mugs of hot coffee. "And it's still only August."

"Don't get too cocky," Franz growled through a mouthful of sausage. "Ivan will hold on to Stalingrad as long as he can, the commissars will make sure of that. Old Uncle Joe Stalin doesn't care how many men it costs. Look at the way they throw wave after wave of attackers at our tanks."

"Exactly. Take the three battalions they sent against us last week. Most of them didn't even have weapons and the officers were so drunk they could barely stand up. Ivan's finished."

"But Franz's got a point," Conrad said, joining in. "Stalin won't want to see his city fall. And they don't always have no weapons. Remember that KV we shot up three days back."

The memory of the mammoth Russian tank silenced them. It had broken down, and Gottfried had pumped shell after shell into it, but they had merely bounced off. Eventually a hatch had opened and the crew emerged, shaken and deafened but uninjured. It had been a sobering experience for the tank crew.

"That was a monster," Gottfried said with a gunner's respect for a well-armored foe. "But it must have a weak spot. I wish I had had more time to examine it."

"Well, I hope someone finds its weak spot before Ivan gets too many of them," Franz said with feeling.

"You guys worry too much," Heinz said, chuckling. "The new Tiger tanks will be here soon. They'll be more than a match for anything Ivan's got. All we need to worry about is Conrad driving us into the river. Ivan's done."

"Speaking of done," Conrad broke in, ignoring the gibe, "breakfast's finished. Eat up. We want to get moving with the rest of the battalion."

Grabbing last hurried mouthfuls of food and gulps of coffee, the crew kicked out the fire, stowed or strapped down anything loose and fired up Lili's engine. Fuel and ammunition had been topped up and orders issued the day before, so they were moving out as the sun appeared on the horizon.

As the tanks of the 16th Panzer Division concentrated for the punch through to the Volga, they reminded Conrad of a herd of grazing prehistoric beasts. Behind them the 3rd and the 60th Motorized Infantry Divisions fell into formation.

This morning, the tank of the corps commander, General Hans Hube, rumbled along in front of Lili. Hube was a brilliant tank commander and his crews loved him. He had lost his right arm in the Great War, but that had not stopped him from leading one of the first motorized units in the new German army. The black metal hand on his false arm made him instantly recognizable.

The sun had barely hauled itself into the sky before a halt was called. A small Fiesler Storch aircraft circled overhead. Droning like an annoyed gnat, it performed a neat landing and bounced to a halt beside Hube's tank. Almost before the propeller had stopped, the pilot jumped down and strode forward. He was tall, middle-aged and broad shouldered. In the already warm morning he was dressed informally in a short-sleeved shirt, the uniform cap of a high-ranking Luftwaffe officer pushed back on his shaven head.

"It's von Richthofen," Gottfried said, peering out of the hull hatch.

All around, tank crews watched in awed silence as the commander-in-chief of the Fourth Air Fleet strode forward and grasped Hube's good hand. Here was the man who had the power to lay waste to entire cities.

"Compliments," Richthofen said perfunctorily.

"General Paulus is worried about his left flank, so the Führer has assigned the entire resources of the Fourth Air Fleet to the Stalingrad front. Today you will have the benefit of twelve hundred aircraft to cripple the Russians."

"And what will the role of this armada be?" Hube asked.

"I know what you want, Hube. You want them all to be assigned to ground support so that your work is done for you and you merely have to drive until you fall into the Volga. Well, you shall have some Stukas but not the fighters. They are too valuable and have been assigned to protect the bombers."

"And what will the bombers' target be?"

"Stalingrad. The city is to be obliterated."

"But you cannot do that in one day," Hube said in an annoyed tone, "even with twelve hundred planes. The city is more than thirty kilometers long and it's a rabbit warren. You won't be doing me any favors by bombing it to rubble."

"It's not my job to do you favors. It's my job to carry out orders."

"So you will slaughter a lot of women and children and clog up the streets with collapsed buildings, robbing my tanks of any ability to maneuver. You will create perfect cover for every mad Russian with an antitank rifle."

Richthofen shrugged dismissively. "I am sure you are up to the task, General. In any case, those are my orders. I am here to acquaint you with them and tell you to make the most of today's attack. I can promise nothing for tomorrow."

With a curt "Heil Hitler," Richthofen strode back to his plane. In a moment it had sprung to life and lifted off into the blue sky. Hube slammed his black fist on the front of his tank. "Damn that arrogant man. These flyboys only think of dogfights and glory. Crawling about the ruins they have so thoughtfully created looking for a squad of Ivans with a rocket launcher would sober them up quickly.

"Well, we must make the most of it. Let's get moving."

As they rumbled forward, Hube's outburst worried Conrad. It was one thing to fight on the open steppe where you could see the enemy coming, but fighting small, hidden groups with antitank rifles in a ruined city promised to be a different matter. Conrad mouthed a silent wish that the Russian defenses would collapse before it came to that.

An hour later, Conrad was distracted by a shadow passing over him. The pale blue sky overhead was alive with black shapes. Wave after wave of Heinkel 111 and Junkers 88 bombers, and tight groups of Stukas droned east, while squadrons of Messerschmitt 109s hovered protectively. How could anything resist such might? Maybe it would be all right, after all.

By noon, Lili had advanced more than forty kilometers unopposed — twelve kilometers ahead lay the Volga and the burning city of Stalingrad. Then, without warning, the tank in front of Conrad exploded. Immediately, Franz locked the left tread and Lili slewed to the side. The division fell into attack formation. Conrad dropped inside the turret and pulled the hatch covers closed, bruising his knee and scraping the skin off his left elbow in the process. It was hot and noisy inside, but there was no time to think about that. As Heinz listened to instructions over the radio, Erich rammed a shell into the breach and Gottfried peered through his sight.

"A battery of 37 mm antiaircraft guns depressed to zero elevation," Heinz relayed from his headset. "That first one was a lucky shot. The Baron says we'll pump a few rounds at them before we move in. Target's just right of that white building."

"I see it," Gottfried replied. "Ready to fire."

"Fire!" Conrad ordered.

The explosion deafened them, and the acrid smell of cordite caught the backs of their throats. Almost before the cannon had finished its violent recoil into the cramped turret, Erich was opening the breech, ejecting the shell case and loading a second one. He was the main reason that Lili's crew had won the rate-of-fire competition in tank school.

After four rounds, the white building was a ruin and there was no sign of life. Slowly the tanks moved forward, until a fountain of dirt erupted in front of Lili and clods and rocks clattered down on the hull.

"Damnation!" Franz shouted. "They're still there."

"Give them another few rounds," Heinz relayed.

Five times, the Baron's tanks poured shells into the antiaircraft position. Five times the tanks began moving forward only to be met by fire from the rubble.

"Those are brave men," Gottfried acknowledged grudgingly.

After the sixth salvo, there was no reply. The tanks moved cautiously ahead, and Conrad dared to open the hatch.

The twisted barrels of the antiaircraft guns pointed uselessly out of piles of shattered bricks and smoldering roof beams. Bodies, some barely recognizable bloody heaps, lay draped like rag dolls over the rubble beside their guns. As Lili ground to a stop, Conrad felt his stomach lurch.

"They're girls!" he said in horror.

"They couldn't even have been out of high school," Gottfried said in disgust as he hauled himself out of the hatch. He was followed by Heinz and Erich, and the three stood in stupefied silence. One body fascinated Heinz. Either the girl had been killed by blast or her wound was on her back, but she lay facing the sky with no visible mark other than a tiny smudge of dirt on her forehead. Her lack of any obvious injury made her more frightful than the torn and mutilated remains around her. She was dressed in shapeless brown combat fatigues and her blond hair was tied back. Her face looked almost peaceful, although her blue eyes were open and stared vacantly at nothing. She didn't look more than sixteen years old.

"How can they send girls into battle?" a shocked Erich asked.

"She looks like my little sister," Heinz said in a choked voice. Abruptly, he knelt and threw up noisily.

It was unforgivable to send girls up against tanks. "They're barbarians," Conrad growled.

"So are we," Gottfried said quietly.

"What?" Conrad asked angrily. "How can you say that? They send untrained schoolgirls to die."

"I agree," Gottfried said, looking at the columns of smoke rising from Stalingrad. "But how many sixteen-year-old girls sitting at home have Richthofen's bombers killed today?"

Conrad looked at the burning city. That was different — wasn't it?

Lili and the other tanks sat in a small grove of oak, walnut and chestnut trees on the banks of the Volga. Huge red-and-black flags with the swastika at the center were laid out in open spaces to let the Stukas know they were friendly. Just a few moments ago, two Me 109s had seen them and performed acrobatic victory rolls above the river to the cheers of the tank crews.

Conrad stood on Lili's turret, scanning the east bank through his binoculars. In front of him, the wide river looked peaceful in the afternoon sun. There was even a small ferry boat chugging slowly across. The far bank stretched away until it merged with the sky.

Asia!

Conrad had grown up on thrilling stories of the medieval Teutonic knights fighting to the last against the Tartar hordes that had swept into Europe from Asia. Now he was avenging them — seven hundred years later. This was his childhood dream come true.

"We've done it!" Heinz shouted gleefully. "The Volga! We've won." His wild enthusiasm exploded into a series of cartwheels around the tank that drew broad grins from his mates.

Erich sat with his legs dangling over the riverbank, chewing on a pear and watching the water rush past below him. Gottfried was on the rear platform of the tank, busily snapping photos with the tiny camera he took everywhere. Even Franz had left the depths of his beloved Lili to smoke a newly made cigarette.

Gottfried snapped a picture of the others relaxing. "It's not over yet — we still have to go there," he said, waving his arm at the columns of smoke that blackened the sky over Stalingrad to the south.

"Hoth's coming up from the south," Heinz said. "He will take the city for us. The Ivans are done."

"Those girls with the antitank guns didn't know they were finished," Franz growled.

The crew's smiles faded. Even Heinz stopped leaping about.

"Sarmatae," Gottfried said thoughtfully.

"What?" Conrad asked.

"Sarmatae. According to Herodotus two thousand years ago, the Sarmatae lived along the Volga. They were related to the Amazons and their women were fearsome warriors."

"Herodotus?"

"The Greek historian. He wrote —"

"I know who Herodotus was," Conrad interrupted. "We did him in school. What I don't know is what his stories have to do with the indoctrinated Communist schoolgirls who almost killed us today."

Gottfried shrugged.

"Too much book learning," Erich said, turning back from the river. "That's what I like about farming. You don't tell how good soil is by reading a book. You run it through your hands. Farming deals with things you can feel."

"And smell," Heinz added with a laugh.

A dull explosion to the south announced yet another trouble spot. The radio crackled into life.

"So, we're not quite finished," Heinz said, jumping onto the tank. "But it won't be long, you mark my words."

As his blond head disappeared down the hatch, the others stretched and climbed aboard. Conrad treated himself to a last, lingering look at Asia before he lowered himself into the turret.

"It's another gun with those soldiers in skirts," Heinz said.

"Are we going to tackle them?" Conrad asked.

"No. Only half the squad is going — to save fuel. We have to stay here and keep an eye on the river. We're to sink any boats we see."

Conrad thought about the ferry boat chugging its way over.

"Franz, get us going. We'd better pull up close to the bank for a good clear shot."

"At the ferry boat?" Heinz asked.

"The order said 'any' boats," Conrad said tersely.

"Yes, but it's full of civilians — women and children —"

"We don't know that," Conrad interrupted. "In any case, do you want it to come back in the dark tonight, full of soldiers in skirts with a load of shells for their guns?"

"No, but —"

"We will obey orders."

Lili rumbled forward until her tracks were at the edge of the bank. The ferry was about two-thirds of the way over, chugging determinedly against the current. The turret swiveled and the gun depressed to find its aim.

"Fire!" Conrad said when a tug on his trouser leg told him everything was ready.

The first shell fell short, sending a spout of water into the air. Through his binoculars, Conrad could see frantic activity on the ferry. Tiny figures scuttled in all directions.

The second shell landed beside the boat, drenching it. Conrad could see figures jumping into the river and being carried downstream by the current. The ferry captain tried desperately to turn his sluggish craft to make it a narrower target.

The third shell exploded on the stern deck of the ferry, hurling stick figures through the air. A moment later, the boat's boiler exploded. In less than thirty seconds, the ferry was gone, leaving an eddy of debris, a few weakly waving figures and several dozen floating bodies — many of them very small and dressed in bright clothes. Conrad lowered his binoculars and closed his eyes. It helped, but the clear air still carried faint screams to his ears.

Was Gottfried right? Were they just as barbaric as their enemy?

No! Terrible things happened in war, that was inevitable. If the Russians were using children to fight or transporting civilians on ferries that could be used to carry soldiers, it was their fault when those civilians were killed. It had to be.

Conrad clambered down into the turret and closed the hatch behind him. The crew sat in silence until they were sure there could be no more screams from the river.

SERGEI

In the doorway of the apartment block, Sergei finds himself looking up at a clear sky. Wave after wave of black shapes roar overhead. All around him explosions echo, smoke and dust clog the air and flames leap. Sergei is shaking with fear. He knows he should do as his mother says and hide in the basement, but this is the most exciting thing that has ever happened. He doesn't want to miss any of it, so he forces down his fear and watches.

The Fascist planes have been coming over all afternoon. At first the bombs fell to the south, around the factories and along the riverbank, but now they are close. Sergei's mother is collecting a few valuables from the apartment in case the building is hit.

A hand falls on Sergei's shoulder and he jumps in terror. Tolstoy's ancient face looms over him. It is time to pay for falling into the turnip allotment. Sergei cringes but no blow falls.

Raising his head, Sergei is amazed to see that instead of the habitual angry frown the old man is weeping. Fascinated, he watches the tears trace their complex way down the deep crevices in Tolstoy's face.

"Hate them!" the old man says, releasing Sergei's shoulder and shaking his fist at the sky. "They are devils. Take a rifle from a dead soldier and kill them all. Your heart must be aflame with hate."

A bomb explodes in the street outside, shattering windows and sending a blast of air through the building. Sergei flees to the basement. Today the war has come to Stalingrad, but all Sergei remembers is that he has escaped a beating.

VASILY

"The great patriotic struggle will continue until the glorious Red Army marches victorious through the ruins of Berlin, past the swinging corpses of the Fascist leaders who began this treacherous war against the Fatherland."

The evening was stifling. Vasily was soaked in sweat, and his skin itched horribly where it was chafed by his coarse uniform. How could the company commissar keep ranting on in this heat? But the man showed no sign of stopping. The commissar's voice sounded tinny and high-pitched through the megaphone, and everyone had heard the same message a hundred times; however, not one of the hundred and forty-four men who formed the three sides of a square around him dared take their eyes off the speaker. Inattention to a political officer could lead to demotion, imprisonment or, during battle, summary execution.

Not that this kept their minds from wandering or stopped the men complaining among themselves.

Cynical old Yevgeny had taken Vasily under his wing and shown him the survival skills that his official training had omitted.

"The earth is your new mother," Yevgeny was fond of saying to the new recruits. "When things get hot, you must return to her. Embrace her as if you are an infant. Never lose your entrenching tool. A few minutes' scraped-up dirt in front of you will stop a bullet. Check every dead German — they have good rations of cheese. And their grenades are better than ours — you can throw them farther."

The old man was rough, but what he said seemed to make sense if Vasily was to stay alive. He was even becoming less shocked at Yevgeny's outspoken criticism of Stalin.

"He doesn't know what he is doing," Yevgeny had said a few days earlier. "Everyone and his pig knew that the Germans were going to attack in the south as soon as summer came, but they still took us by surprise. Now they are damn nearly on the Volga, and what do we do? Sit here on our arses and listen to how Comrade Stalin is going to fight to the last drop of our blood. 'On to Berlin' — Ha! We'll be lucky to see Kharkov again before we're all floating facedown in the Volga or being marched to some Fascist labor camp."

Vasily's father would say such negativity was wrong, unforgivable. "It can undermine everyone's will to resist the invader. Vasily, you must report that man to the commissar for reeducation."

But Vasily didn't report Yevgeny.

Vasily might despise Yevgeny's political weakness and have little in common with him, but there was a deep bond within the squad: any soldier's life often depended on his close comrades. So it was not a good idea to anger anyone who might soon have the power of life and death over you. Besides, Vasily suspected that Yevgeny's practical advice might be important one day.

Although Vasily would never dream of saying it aloud, Yevgeny was voicing things that Vasily had been wondering about. Why *were* they sitting idly listening to speeches while the Fascists rolled toward the Volga? All ten thousand of the 13th Guards Division were in or around Kamyshin now. What were they waiting for? True, replacements for those lost in the train attack had not yet arrived, and one in ten had no rifle, but the 13th was still a potent fighting force. Vasily was sure they could help halt the Fascist drive to the Volga — if only they were given a chance. Vasily believed that Comrade Stalin had something special in mind for the Guards, but that didn't make the waiting any easier.

Despite the inaction, Vasily was happy. At first the older soldiers had laughed at his youthful enthusiasm and, he suspected, been envious that he had been issued a submachine gun. But his loneliness and isolation disappeared one night in the barracks where they spent their precious spare time, gambling and drinking. There was an old piano in the corner, and Vasily had begun to play one of the old songs his father had taught him. The piano was horribly out of tune, but a small crowd had soon gathered. Embarrassed, Vasily had stopped playing.

"Go on," Yevgeny had ordered.

Soon everyone was standing, arm in arm, singing lustily as Vasily played. Lively songs had everyone stamping his feet and belting out the lyrics. Slow songs produced tears in the eyes of his hard-bitten comrades.

Vasily's mind drifted back to the present as the commissar droned to a close and the men dispersed. Now came one of the rare times Vasily could call his own — the short break before the men mustered for dinner. Most spent the time in idle conversation or at card games, but Vasily spent it on his own. He had found a spot among the willows along the river where it was cool and quiet. The bulging roots of an old tree formed a natural seat where he could rest, write letters to his father or just watch the water — water that had flowed from the Valday Hills north of Moscow, east almost to the Ural Mountains before it reached his feet. After it had passed, it would flow beside the great factory city of Stalingrad and south to the Caspian Sea, before lapping the exotic shores of Persia.

How could the Fascists have believed that they could successfully conquer such a huge nation, Vasily wondered as he walked toward the river. Russia was timeless, immortal. She had swallowed Napoleon, the master of Europe, and spat out the frozen remnants of his army in a single year. This invader was taking longer, but Vasily absolutely knew that the result would be the same.

He stopped. Someone was sitting in *his* spot — he could see a shoulder sticking out.

As Vasily watched, the figure stretched and stood up. Long black hair fell over the brown uniform collar. He knew there were women in the Red Army — the commissar had devoted several lectures to their heroic contribution — and everyone was equal, so why shouldn't women be allowed to kill Fascists just like men? Still, it was a surprise.

The woman turned — Vasily gasped. He had expected an older, battle-hardened face like those of the weather-beaten peasant women he had seen laboring in the fields. Instead, he was face to face with an angel. She was not much older than he — and beautiful. Her black hair, high cheekbones and olive skin suggested some Asian heritage, but her features were more delicate than the Siberian soldiers Vasily had come across. As he gaped, the girl surveyed him coolly with eyes as black as her hair.

"Can I help you, Comrade?" she asked.

"No. Yes. I mean, that's my tree." Vasily stumbled awkwardly over the simplest thoughts and words. He felt color rising in his cheeks.

"Your tree? Do you own many around here?"

"No. I mean, I don't own any trees. It's just that this is where I usually come to think."

The girl nodded. "A thoughtful soldier — you are a rarity. But that is good. I wouldn't want to think you were an unreconstructed landowner from before the revolution."

She said it without a trace of irony in her voice, but Vasily had the impression she was teasing him. He could think of nothing to say.

"I am leaving, so you can have your tree back." The girl bent to pick up her rifle, a reliable and accurate M91/30. The bolt had been specially altered so loading would not interfere with the long black telescopic sight mounted on top.

"You're a sniper!" Vasily exclaimed.

The girl smiled. It was an odd smile, with only one side of her mouth, as if she wasn't certain whether it was worth committing her whole face to the activity. But the black eyes sparkled, and Vasily felt his knees go weak.

"Sniper Yelena Pavlova, assigned to B Platoon, H Company, 52nd Rifle Battalion. At your service." She bowed very slightly in Vasily's direction.

Again, he wasn't certain if she was being ironic. Then he realized what she had said. "That ... that's my platoon."

"Then we are to be comrades in arms." Again that enigmatic smile. "What is your name, Comrade?"

"Rifleman Vasily Sarayev. I'm from Moscow."

"Moscow. I've heard of that place. Perhaps I will go there one day — after I have been to Berlin."

"Wh-where are *you* from?" Vasily stammered.

"I am from over the Ural Mountains — a small village you have never heard of near a town you wouldn't know," Yelena replied, her ironic smile firmly in place.

"Wha-what's it called?"

"The village has no name. People just call it 'the village on the edge of the forest.'"

Cradling her rifle, Yelena turned to go. Vasily's mouth couldn't form the simplest words, yet he wished more than anything to keep Yelena talking.

"I — I have heard of that place," he gasped.

Yelena turned back, a flicker of interest on her face. She inclined her head questioningly.

Vasily felt as if a steel band were tightening around his chest. He could barely draw enough oxygen into his lungs. What stupid thing had he blurted out? How could he possibly have heard of a place known only as 'the village on the edge of the forest'? Yet it *had* sparked a memory.

For what seemed like an age, Vasily stood frozen in front of this beautiful woman. Suddenly, an idea exploded in his head. He remembered the folk tales the old men used to tell when he was a child.

"Yes," he said. "Once there was a village on the edge of a dark forest. It was there that the old peasant tricked the bear."

A puzzled frown crossed Yelena's face. "Bear?"

The tale unfolded in Vasily's mind like a patchwork quilt. Once he began, one event followed another as naturally as day and night. His breathing eased, his voice became firmer and the nervous sweat dried on his forehead. It was as if the story told itself.

"One day, the old peasant farmer ventured into the forest. After a short while, he found a clearing that was ideal for planting vegetables. He had just prepared the land and planted a nice crop of turnips when a huge bear ambled out of the trees."

The frown left Yelena's face. She leaned against a tree and watched Vasily closely.

"'Get out of my forest,' the bear said, 'or I shall tear you apart.'

"'Oh, but, Mikhailo Ivanovich,' the peasant said, using the bear's proper name. 'I have just planted a wonderful field of turnips. If you let me tend them, we can share. You can have the beautiful green tops of the turnips and I will take the roots from the ground.'

"This sounded like a good idea to the bear, so he agreed.

"When the turnips were ready, the bear and the peasant returned. The peasant broke off the tops and gave them to the bear. He then dug up all the turnips and loaded them onto his cart to take to market and sell.

"The bear ate the turnip tops. 'These are bitter,' he said. 'Can I try one of the roots?'

"'Certainly,' said the the peasant, handing over a turnip.

"The bear bit into it. 'These are sweet!' he exclaimed. 'You have the best bit. You tricked me.'

"'That was our agreement,' the peasant said. As the bear moved toward him threateningly, he quickly added, 'but I want to be fair. Next time, I will take the top part and you can have the roots.'

"The bear agreed. The next season, the old man planted a field of rye —"

"And he took the grain in the tops and left the poor old bear with the useless bitter roots!" Yelena shouted gleefully.

"And ever since then, bears and men have been mortal enemies."

"That's a good story, Rifleman Vasily Sarayev. Thank you." Yelena shouldered her rifle. "But I don't think it happened near my village." With a smile, she walked off through the trees.

Vasily watched her go with an idiotic grin on his face. He had never spoken so much to a girl in his entire life — and she had seemed to enjoy it. His legs felt suddenly weak.

This war was turning out to be even more of an adventure than he had expected.

DAY 88

STALINGRAD

Monday, September 14, 1942

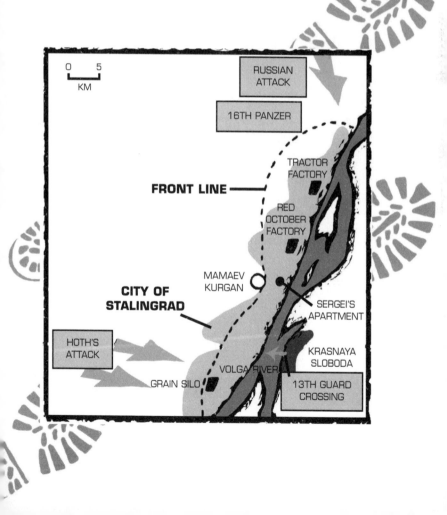

RUSSIAN ATTACK

16TH PANZER

FRONT LINE

TRACTOR FACTORY

RED OCTOBER FACTORY

MAMAEV KURGAN

CITY OF STALINGRAD

SERGEI'S APARTMENT

HOTH'S ATTACK

KRASNAYA SLOBODA

VOLGA RIVER

GRAIN SILO

13TH GUARD CROSSING

0   5
KM

CONRAD

Conrad didn't feel like eating the meager cold breakfast Erich was dishing out beside Lili — the knot in his stomach was destroying his appetite, as it always did before a battle. Yesterday, reconnaissance had spotted a buildup of Russian tanks. Today they would attack, to relieve the pressure on their comrades in the ruins of Stalingrad to the south.

Conrad sauntered through the predawn chill to examine the Russian prisoners being held under guard nearby. That was another sure sign that an attack was coming — the flow of deserters always increased before an offensive. The three men in front of Conrad stood under a small oak tree, stamping their feet and slapping their arms to keep warm. They were unshaven, dirty and cowed.

"They don't look like soldiers at all, do they?" Gottfried had come up beside Conrad. The pair regarded the pitiful trio and wondered how such men had managed to bring the mightiest army in the world to a halt, even temporarily.

"They look like poor dirt farmers," Conrad observed.

One of the prisoners glanced up. He had a square, unshaven face heavily marked with smallpox scars. "Yes. Yes. Farmer," he said in broken German. "War bad. Stalin kaput. Cigarette?" The other two men lifted their heads hopefully at the request.

Behind Conrad, Lili's engine fired into life. Hurriedly, he thrust a handful of cigarettes at the prisoners and turned away.

"They're little better than animals," Conrad said in a low voice.

"And we might end up exactly the same way," Gottfried added. Conrad was about to argue, but Gottfried strode ahead to Lili and began stowing equipment. Ten minutes later, Conrad was standing in Lili's turret, guiding them through a thin screen of trees to the division's other tanks. Before them, low marshy land exuded wisps of mist that hung in the air like tattered cotton balls. Behind the mist, bare fields rose gradually to a crest over which the Russians would appear.

For a long time, little happened. The sun rose on Conrad's right and its warmth burned off the mist.

"They're going to be sitting ducks as they cross that ridge ahead," Gottfried said.

"Which won't do us much good if they're those damned MV tanks," Erich grumbled.

"They don't have many of them," Heinz contributed cheerfully.

"I hope you're right," Gottfried said.

Everyone lapsed into silence. They all knew how important this day would be. To the south, brutal battles were under way in the center of Stalingrad for control of Mamaev Kurgan, the highest hill in the city, and the nearby sprawling complex of the Red October Factory. If the Russian attack here succeeded, reserves would have to be drawn away from the city to support the 16th Division, and both the hill and the factory would not be held. For Conrad it was also personal: it was Hoth's tanks that were advancing toward Red October. Success here today would help Josef.

"Here they come!" Gottfried shouted.

Conrad dropped into the body of the tank, pulling the hatch closed after him. Hurriedly, he tore off two pieces of cotton batten, crumpled them and stuffed them into his ears. It was about to become very noisy.

A line of black shapes was growing on the brow of the hill. Shells were throwing up fountains of earth across the field.

"Fire when ready," Conrad said quietly.

Inside the tank was surprisingly hot, and Conrad felt prickles of sweat breaking out on his skin. The numerous scratches he had picked up as he had moved around Lili's confined space began to sting. Why wasn't Gottfried firing? The hill was alive with tanks and exploding shells. Russian infantry were beginning to work their way between the tanks, tiny dots, still too far away to do any damage.

Conrad was relieved to see that none of the dark shapes rumbling across the ridge were the dreaded MVs. Very few were even T–34s. Most were a type he hadn't seen before, smaller and with a higher profile. That would at least make them easier targets.

Lili's cannon exploded. On the hillside, one of the strange new tanks slewed to the side and burst into flames.

"Good shot!" Conrad exclaimed as Erich ejected the casing and rammed home a fresh shell. Heinz got Lili's machine guns stuttering out a stream of bullets that fell among the Russian infantry.

The noise was deafening and men were dying in great numbers, but Conrad felt disconnected. The tanks exploding and burning on the hillside were distant toys, not vehicles filled with people, and it was hard to imagine that the stick figures crumpling to the ground around them were human. Even the Russian shells exploding near Lili only made distant, deep thumps that at most threw branches or rocks onto the tank's armor.

Lili's cannon exploded, and a dark mass of earth erupted beside an enemy tank.

"Damn," Gottfried cursed. "He swung away at the last second."

Lili's crew worked on in silence until the Russians retreated, dragging their wounded comrades with them. The burning hulks of tanks dotted the cratered hillside, and smaller irregular shapes marked the positions of bodies.

Conrad threw open the hatch and took a deep breath. The acrid smell of smoke, explosives and gasoline mingled incongruously with the fresh smell of sap from the shattered trees.

"So much for them," Heinz said gleefully as he opened the side hatch.

"They'll be back," Conrad said. "This is just the beginning. Clear out the old shell casings, get ready for the next attack and then grab a smoke."

As the crew busied themselves, Conrad's sense of unreality returned. He was amazed each time the crew did what he told them. Didn't they know he was just Josef's kid brother? He had always been Josef's little brother tagging along with the older kids, always being told to do this or not do that or to go away and not bother them, yet here he was in charge of a tank.

"They are American tanks." Gottfried's voice came from inside the hull. "Shermans, I think they're called. They must have come across the Atlantic, around Scandinavia to Murmansk and then across Russia to here."

"Just to be blown up! Well, I say keep them coming," Heinz said cheerfully. "They are much easier to destroy than the T-34s."

"That they are," Gottfried agreed, "and it looks as if we are going to get another chance."

Moving shapes were again appearing on the far ridge.

"Here we go," Conrad said as the first shells exploded among the trees.

Seven times that day, the Russian soldiers and tanks crested the ridge and swarmed across the field. Seven times they were driven back, leaving behind burned-out hulks and still bodies. Seventy-two tanks were destroyed by the 16th Division. Gottfried's tally had been three. Not a single German soldier or tank had been drawn away from the fighting in Stalingrad.

"Shooting fish in a barrel," Heinz reflected contentedly, as the low evening sun softened the harsh scene of desolation.

The tanks had been drawn back when it became obvious that the Russians weren't coming again. Conrad and the others were sitting by Lili's tracks, a coffeepot heating on a small fire. They were all in a good mood after the day's success.

"The Ivans never seem to learn," Gottfried observed, "and the Yanks make lousy tanks."

"But they make good chocolate," Heinz said. The five tired but well-fed crew chuckled at their good fortune. Not only had the Russians been supplied with American tanks but the bodies strewn across the hillside, instead of carrying the usual Russian rations — black, coarse rye bread; tough sausage; hard, small red potatoes and wilted cabbage — had been a gold mine of treats: British tinned beets, soup cubes and sweet biscuits, and American hard candy and Hershey bars. Spiced sausage, a hard-boiled egg each, chocolate bars, sugar cubes, and the last of the apples from a nearby orchard provided as good a dinner as the men had had since the campaign began.

"Once we are finished here," Heinz continued through a mouthful of delicious chocolate sweetness, "we should invade Switzerland."

"No," Erich said, "not enough good farmland — too many mountains."

Conrad laughed. "And not good tank country. We're better off on the open steppe."

"So why are we fighting in the streets of Stalingrad?" Gottfried asked, launching into what had become his favorite topic. "It makes no sense. Tanks are not designed for street fighting. We've had it easy up until now, but our turn is coming. Just you wait."

"But the city is almost ours," Heinz objected. "We're only a few hundred meters from the river. One more attack and we will control the river crossings. The Ivans won't be able to bring in reinforcements or supplies. They'll have to evacuate the city."

"Maybe, but if I had a Reichsmark for every time I have heard that we are on the brink of victory, I'd be a rich man. Look at that battle for the grain silo. It took Hoth days to smash his way into it. He lost hundreds of men and several tanks — and what did they find when the pile of rubble was secure? Fifty bodies! Fifty Ivans with a couple of machine guns and some grenades held off an entire infantry division with tank, artillery and air support. Every pile of rubble becomes a fortress that has to be attacked. It's a defender's dream. And they're all fanatics. We used to think those schoolgirls were an exception, but they're all like that."

"Sure, it's a lot tougher than we thought," Heinz persisted, "and Ivan isn't as close to finished as we would like, but we have to keep going."

"Why?" Gottfried leaned forward aggressively. "Stalingrad is of no value. We're on the Volga, so we can cut traffic along it. The Luftwaffe has destroyed the city's industry. We could just sit back and lob shells in whenever Ivan looks to be rebuilding. Then he would have to live in the godforsaken place, not us."

Heinz sat in silence.

"I'll tell you why." Gottfried answered his own question. "Because it's become a personal vendetta between Stalin and Hitler. One cannot give up the city that bears his name, and the other won't rest until he has taken it. And we're caught like rats in between."

"The Führer knows what he is doing!" Heinz exclaimed excitedly. "Once Stalingrad falls, the war will be over."

"Don't be so naive," Gottfried hissed.

"Enough!" Conrad broke in. "Yes, it is difficult. Yes, it is bloody. But our orders are to take the city, so take it we will. Save your energy for fighting Ivan. Gottfried's right, we have had it easy so far. It's time we did our bit in the city."

Conrad's tone was harsher than he intended. It was annoying that his crew was arguing, but only because they voiced his own growing doubts. He knew that a tank commander far away from the high command on a battlefield in Russia could never see the whole picture, but things were not working out as he had hoped. Conrad was also worried about Josef already fighting in the city. Their hope of being at home on Christmas leave was becoming less likely by the day.

"It's not the soldiers, it's the rats," Franz contributed. "If our tanks stop for more than an hour or two, the damnable beasts gnaw through the insulation and short out the wiring. I never thought a rat, even a Russian one, could stop a tank."

"Exactly." Gottfried leaped back into the conversation. "Half our tanks are out of commission because of rats or because they are damaged or worn out and we can't get spare parts. Those Russians were on the verge of collapse a month ago — but they're still there, and so are we."

"They are wearing down faster than we are." Nothing could dent Heinz's optimism. "The Führer has called for Stalingrad to fall tomorrow."

"My apologies." Gottfried sarcastically doffed his cap. "If the Führer says it will be so, then I am stupid to doubt. I am sure it was because of my doubts that the city didn't fall when the Führer last said it would!"

"Enough," Conrad broke in. "Today was a success. Let's just enjoy that. Tomorrow will look after itself — there's no use arguing over what might happen. Now, give me another of those chocolate bars and a cup of coffee. Let's enjoy life while we can."

SERGEI

The bomb that lands in the street the day he escaped Tolstoy is only the first. In the following three weeks, many others fall, reducing his apartment block and every other large building in the city to a ruin.

Although it is night as Sergei emerges from the cellar that is now home, countless fires make it as bright as day. Above him, the sky is busy with red and green flares, arcing tracer bullets and the fiery paths of rockets. Explosions and the pop of small-arms fire echo in every direction. The air is sickly sweet with the smell of decomposing bodies.

None of this bothers Sergei. It is just a game, bigger and more dangerous than the one he used to play in the courtyard, but still a game. It started with sneaking out, trying to catch glimpses of the Fascist tanks or the soldiers in their odd coal-scuttle helmets; but that has lost its novelty. Now the game is to find food in abandoned buildings or on dead bodies. Tonight he is going to dig for forgotten turnips in Tolstoy's allotment.

Darting among the shadows, Sergei makes his way over the rubble. There is little that hasn't been scavenged, but sometimes the daytime bombing turns up something that has been missed.

Lying flat, Sergei scrabbles in the dirt. It is hard work and he occasionally digs up unpleasant surprises; but tonight, half an hour's work rewards Sergei with the hard, round shape of a turnip. He has almost uncovered it when a voice, frighteningly close to his left ear says, "This is my turnip patch."

Sergei has not seen Tolstoy for more than a week and has assumed that he has either managed to escape across the river or been killed. He suspects the latter, since the old man appeared to have gone mad and often wandered around in the open during a raid, cursing the planes.

Sergei turns his head to see the wrinkled face leering at him from less than a meter away.

"It's not nice to steal," the face says. "But then you boys were always trouble. What're you going to do with that turnip?"

"Eat it," Sergei replies, puzzled. "Mother will make some soup. You can have some."

Tolstoy lets out a dry laugh. "I don't need turnip soup. But you do. Build up your strength to kill Fascists. A dead Fascist for every turnip. That's my price if you want to steal from my plot."

"Okay. Yes. Agreed." Sergei is ready to say anything to escape.

"Good boy."

Sergei leaps to his feet and, clutching the turnip to his chest, sprints for the basement steps. Behind him he can hear Tolstoy's insane laughter.

VASILY

Vasily was terrified as he jumped down from the back of the filthy truck in the late-afternoon sunlight. His legs felt weak and his mouth was dry. Beads of sweat trickled down his face and his stomach felt queasy.

His symptoms were partly due to exhaustion — the 13th Guards had been traveling south nonstop for the past three days. Vasily's only breaks from the bone-jarring monotony had been when the truck's radiator boiled over in the heat or when he flung himself into the ditch as Messerschmitts roared in to strafe the column. The division's route from Kamyshin to this riverbank grove of poplar trees at Krasnaya Sloboda was lined with the rotting bodies of ungainly pack camels and broken equipment; but now the column had arrived, and that accounted for most of Vasily's fear.

Through the trees and across the Volga lay Stalingrad and the Fascist invaders who were within an ace of pushing the Red Army into the river. Vasily could hear the *crump* of explosions from the battle he was about to join and see the angry glow of the burning city reflected off the low, scattered clouds. For months he had been looking forward to this moment, imagining the glory of it, but now all he could think of was being shot or blown apart by a bomb or shell.

All around Vasily, men milled in confusion as officers distributed ammunition and rations of bread, sausage and sugar. Vasily managed to grab round magazines of ammunition and some food, which he hurriedly stuffed into his pack.

"Better take some grenades. They'll be of most use where we're going." Yelena stood to one side, calmly watching the distribution.

"Why don't you have any, then?" Vasily asked defensively. Every time his path had crossed Yelena's in the past month, he had felt the same confusion. One reason was her disconcerting habit of saying one thing while flashing that smile that seemed to say she meant something entirely different. The other reason was that the mere sight of her made Vasily weak.

"I have all I need here." Yelena patted the rifle held in the crook of her arm.

"So have I," said Vasily, clumsily indicating his SG43.

"Suit yourself. How fast does that thing fire?"

"More than five rounds a second," Vasily replied, glad to be distracted from his fear. "How many shots can you get off in that time?"

Yelena ignored his cheeky question. "And how many rounds does the magazine hold?"

"Seventy."

"So, if you are going down into a dark cellar full of Fascists, you have about fourteen seconds to make sure they are all dead? I'd rather lob a grenade down before I go in — just to make sure." Again that smile.

Vasily tried to remain calm, but suddenly seventy bullets didn't seem that many. Quickly, he grabbed four grenades and tucked them into his belt. When he turned around, Yelena was nowhere to be seen.

"Come on! No time to waste." Nikolai was forming up the squad. "We have a boat to catch. They need us on the other side of the river."

Vasily and the others followed their commander through the trees, directed by a rough wooden sign with "Ferry" crudely painted on it. Vasily was never certain of his legs — they seemed to have a mind of their own and threatened to turn him around and carry him away from the terror ahead. It took all his concentration to put one foot in front of the other.

The first sight of Stalingrad as the trees opened up was fearful; the whole city was on fire. For kilometers in either direction, ruined buildings spewed flames. White and red tracer bullets cut through the threatening clouds of smoke that obscured the setting sun. Artillery and small-arms fire echoed over the wide expanse of water. Even Yevgeny was awed into silence. It was like an ancient holy man's fevered vision of hell.

In front of them, an absurd collection of vessels lay along the riverbank. Two gunboats looked almost military, but the rest were tugs, barges, fishing smacks and rowing boats.

"All right!" Nikolai shouted. "This one's ours. In you get."

The vessel he indicated was low, open and painted white. Six marines in blue-and-white-striped shirts sat with oars held up over the water. Vasily guessed the boat had once been a lifeboat on a large ship.

The squad scrambled in over the gunwales, settling wherever they could. The precious heavy machine gun was loaded with a box of ammunition. Yelena settled in the bow. Nikolai sat at the stern and immediately began flicking his lighter. Vasily found himself seated to one side, between two of the rowers. On a command from the shore, they were pushed off and the marines dipped their oars in the rushing current.

At first the strange crossing was uneventful. The gunfire from the city and the heavy chug of the tugs' and gunboats' engines sounded a long way off, and Vasily could hear the water lapping against the boat's side and the creaking of the oars working in unison. Most of the soldiers were reluctant to look at the inferno they were heading for, but Vasily was mesmerized. He could barely believe that men and women could be fighting and dying in the fires and smoke. Stalingrad was nothing but ruins.

A new fear edged into Vasily's mind. What if he was a coward? That would be worse than dying. His father, the army and the nation had put their trust in him.

What if he failed them? Even worse, what if he did something stupid or cowardly in front of Yelena?

A German shell exploded in a fountain of water in front of one of the gunboats. As if that was a signal, a cacophony of artillery, machine guns and mortars opened up. The surface of the river seethed. Instinctively, Vasily lowered his head so his helmet was tilted toward the source of the enemy fire. It was a futile gesture — his helmet wouldn't stop anything being thrown at him — but it made him feel a little better. Now his view was of the water, lit by flashes of exploding shells and the fires on the far bank. The silver bellies of stunned fish glinted in the eerie light.

All around, boats were being hit and wounded men were screaming before they sank beneath the dark water. Spray from exploding shells drenched Vasily and his comrades, yet through it all the marines kept up a steady rhythm.

"Damn them. Couldn't they wait till nightfall so we'd at least have cover of darkness," Yevgeny complained, finding his voice. Nikolai ignored the comment, concentrated on fiddling with his lighter.

A white face with dead staring eyes loomed up in front of Vasily and bumped disconsolately against the side of the boat. Vasily jerked his head up just in time to see the burst of machine-gun fire strike the far side of the boat. One of the marines and two soldiers from his squad died instantly. The boat slewed sideways.

"Damn them," Yevgeny repeated, but whether his curse was directed at the German machine gunner or his own officers wasn't clear. No one had a chance to find out. A bullet hit Yevgeny in the temple, and he collapsed over the machine gun, blood pumping out into a puddle with the water at the bottom of the boat. Another man gasped and died at Vasily's feet.

The marines struggled to regain control of the vessel. The dead were unceremoniously bundled over the side. The machine gunner stood up and attempted to haul Yevgeny's body off his weapon. The boat rocked alarmingly. The marines screamed at the man to sit down — he ignored them. The rocking became worse as Yevgeny's body and the heavy machine gun lurched from side to side. The gunwale beside Vasily dipped and a small tidal wave swept into the boat. They were going to sink. Despite the death and destruction in the boat, Vasily was horrified by the thought of being thrown into the water. He wasn't a good swimmer, and with all his equipment he'd probably sink, joining the dead fish and pale corpses.

A gunshot exploded beside Vasily's ear. The machine gunner looked surprised, dropped Yevgeny's body, clutched his stomach and collapsed in a heap. The boat's motion settled. Vasily looked around to see Nikolai returning his pistol to its holster. "Get them over the side!" he yelled. "And use your helmets to bail!"

Vasily and another soldier struggled to dump the limp bodies into the river. Reluctantly, he removed his helmet and began throwing the bloody water after them.

Vasily's boat had almost reached shore and was partly protected by a high bank above a wide gravel strip. The Germans were concentrating their fire on the vessels still in midstream. Vasily looked at the chaos around him. In the bottom of the boat, the machine gun lay on its side, bloody water sloshing around it.

Four marines continued to row. The fifth groaned as he tried to stem the flow of blood from a jagged hole in his thigh. Vasily was in shock. In ten minutes, five of his squad had been killed. The surviving rifleman sat by the machine gun, staring doggedly ahead. Nikolai was in the stern, his face set, his lighter nowhere to be seen. Yelena, huddled in the curve of the prow, holding her precious rifle close to her chest, had not moved a muscle for the entire voyage. As Vasily stared, Yelena met his eyes and smiled. Then the boat ground onto the shore.

Nikolai was first out into the knee-deep water. "Come on!" he shouted. "The faster we reach cover, the longer we will live."

The survivors piled ashore among other men of the 13th Guards. Vasily recognized some units from his company. A commissar with a bloodstained rag wrapped around his head was ordering them forward. Nikolai approached him and asked for orders.

The commissar looked over the remains of the squad and pointed to the ruined buildings on top of the riverbank. "Go that way and kill Fascists," he said simply. "You should find them in about two hundred meters. Grab some grenades on the way, as many as each man can carry. And leave the machine gun. You'll be too close to the enemy for it to be any use tonight."

Nikolai saluted.

"Oh, and one other thing," the commissar said. "If you take one step back, you will be shot." Without returning Nikolai's salute, the commissar moved on to another group of confused soldiers. Behind him, a truck carrying a Katyusha rocket launcher reversed out from the shelter of the bank. With earsplitting screams, the sixteen rockets left the launcher and shot over the city as the truck retreated back to the safety of the bank.

Ducking low, Nikolai led them up a shallow gully. Other members of B platoon followed. Vasily was aware of bullets smacking into the earth bank above his head, but they meant nothing.

At the head of the gully, an officer was directing men to right and left. He sent Nikolai and the others toward a red-brick building whose ruined and pock-marked walls stood higher than those around it.

"The Fascists are there," the officer said. "If they gain control of that building, they will be able to fire directly onto the beach. You must stop them."

No complex strategy here: defend that building to the death.

Nikolai led the way in a zigzag crouching run toward the building. He darted from patch of cover to patch of cover. During each run, several men fell to the machine-gun fire coming from the red-brick building, joining the scattered corpses from earlier attacks.

Vasily noticed Yelena hesitating. Was she scared too?

"Are you all right?" Vasily shouted across at her.

Yelena ignored him. She was staring fixedly at the building in front of them. She must have been frozen with terror. Vasily worked his way over until he was lying beside her. "Are you all right?"

"The machine gun is at the third window from the left on the second floor," she said without looking at Vasily. "They have it well sited. I can't get a clear shot. I want you to fire an entire magazine at the window." The instructions were delivered in a flat voice. Vasily never considered disobeying them. Settling himself in the rubble as best he could, he pointed his submachine gun at the window and pulled the trigger. The cylindrical magazine emptied remarkably quickly. Vasily had no idea if he had hit anyone, but he could see puffs of brick dust around the dark opening.

"Again," Yelena ordered.

As Vasily changed magazines, he was aware of Yelena lying, with unnatural stillness beside him. Halfway through his second magazine Yelena's rifle cracked and a gray body lurched out the window and fell to the ground below.

"You got him!" Vasily yelled exultantly.

"Wait!" Yelena ordered quietly as she smoothly worked the rifle's bolt. "They always have a backup gunner."

Vasily stared at the black window. He thought he saw a flicker of movement in its depth. Yelena's rifle barked. An arm appeared and dangled limply over the windowsill.

"That should hold them for a while," Yelena said. "Now we move."

Without question, Vasily followed her in a crouching run toward the red building. With calm efficiency, she had killed two men and saved dozens of lives. And he had thought she was scared. He would have followed her anywhere.

The pair piled through a jagged hole in the wall of the building. Inside, Nikolai crouched behind the bullet riddled boiler of some long-destroyed piece of machinery.

"Where do you want us, Commander?" Yelena asked.

Nikolai shrugged. "You heard the commissar. The Fascists hold the far side of the building and most of the floor above. If we hold on, they lose. If we don't, they win, but it won't matter to us, we'll be long dead by then. You are a sniper — take the kid with you and kill as many Fascists as you can. Good luck."

Yelena nodded and crawled off to the right. Vasily followed her. Oddly, now that he might have only minutes before death, his fear had vanished. His mind was unnaturally alert and he heard every rifle crack, shell explosion and bullet's ricochet as if it were the only noise in a silent room. War was very strange.

Behind him he heard Nikolai say, "Welcome to Stalingrad."

DAY 131

BATTLES IN THE RUBBLE

Tuesday, October 27, 1942

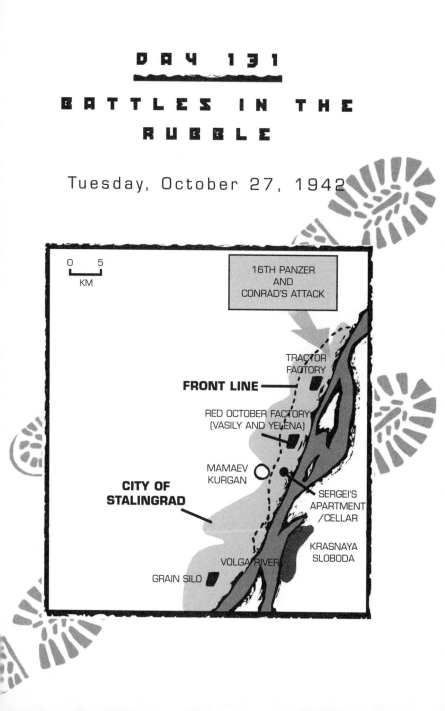

CONRAD

"Fire!" Conrad yelled. The cannon thundered and recoiled violently into the turret. The wall of a house at the far end of the rubble-strewn street disappeared in a cloud of smoke and dust.

"A hit!" Gottfried shouted bitterly. "I thought that house was going to get away from us."

All morning it had been the same. Lili, separated from the rest of the division, had been maneuvering through the suburbs, destroying buildings and strongpoints that threatened to hold up the infantry advance. It was hot, tiring, dangerous work and, as Gottfried never failed to point out, "not what tanks were designed for."

As Lili lurched over the rubble, men from the 3rd Motorized Infantry Division cautiously searched the ruins on either side. The soldiers were loaded down with the standard-issue tubular mess kit, rolled greatcoat, backpack and ammunition pouch. Equipment dangled from their belts — some had pistols, water canteens and shapeless bags of one sort or another, but all had bayonets and as many grenades as they had been able to find.

Grenades were the most useful weapon in this house-to-house fighting, although some soldiers preferred the rare machine pistols. One soldier toward the front carried a flamethrower and, from time to time, let jets of burning, jellied fuel sweep into suspicious-looking rooms and doorways. Behind Lili, soldiers stumbled along carrying heavy machine guns, antitank rocket launchers and field radios.

Progress was painfully slow. The Russian defense consisted of small squads, sometimes with an antitank gun, snipers in the taller ruins and the terrifying T-34 tanks, buried to the turret in rubble. Every shadow could harbor sudden death. Every nerve was stretched to breaking point.

As Conrad peered ahead through a slit in Lili's armor, a soldier in front of the tank slumped to the ground. His comrades immediately dropped into whatever cover they could find. Conrad had not heard the shot above Lili's engine, but the soldiers on the street were pointing at a group of windows in a gutted department store to the right. Several held up four fingers.

"Swivel right thirty degrees," Conrad ordered. "There's a sniper on the fourth floor. Let's put a shell in to discourage him."

As the turret ground around, Erich loaded a shell and Gottfried raised the gun to aim. It's like trying to kill an ant with a sledgehammer, Conrad thought. Besides, if the sniper's any good, he'll be long gone to a new location where he can pick off another man. Conrad tried to find a more comfortable position for his cramped and aching limbs. Silently, he wished he were Josef's size.

"Fire when ready," Conrad ordered.

Again the explosion of the gun reverberated around the tank, and a section of wall between two windows of the store crashed into the street below. Satisfied that the sniper had at least been discouraged, the soldiers continued along the street.

Conrad's eyes strained to spot danger first, although there was little chance that he would see anything through the narrow turret slit before the hyper-alert soldiers on the ground did. He didn't know how much more he could take. Already today he had seen dozens of men killed at very close range. He was glad to be relatively safe from snipers and machine guns, but he hated not being able to see around the next corner. He missed the wide-open steppe, where he could ride with the hatch open and see for great distances in all directions. Gottfried was right — this was no way to use tanks.

The soldier carrying the flamethrower suddenly jerked back against a wall as machine-gun bullets from a side street caught his fuel pack. Twitching madly, the burning figure lurched out into the road in a grotesque dance until one of his comrades put him out of his agony with a burst of automatic fire.

"Damn it. Here we go again," Gottfried complained wearily as the turret swiveled to fire down the side street when Lili passed. "Another suicidal Ivan with a machine gun."

Ahead, soldiers were scurrying to find covered positions and return fire. Others were clambering through holes in walls in attempts to outflank the enemy. Bursts of machine-gun fire scattered brick chips and kept the infantrymen's heads low.

"Ready!" Conrad yelled as they neared the corner. Franz hunched over the controls, peering at the rubble ahead; Gottfried stared intently through his gun sight, waiting for the target to swing into view; Heinz clutched the handle of the turret's machine gun; and Erich crouched to one side, ready to remove the spent shell casing and ram a fresh one into the breach.

Lili's tracks were just clearing the corner of the side street when the house wall overhead exploded. Large blocks of masonry clanged down on the tank, and her crew instinctively ducked. Shrugging off pieces of wall, Lili rumbled out into the intersection.

Gottfried was the first to see it. He gasped but never moved his eye from the gun sight. A T-34 sat about two hundred and fifty meters along the side street. It was buried hull deep in the rubble, with only its squat turret showing. Fortunately for Lili and her crew, it had just fired the shell at the second floor of the building, so its evil-looking long cannon was too high to fire effectively at the tank.

"Go," Conrad yelled unnecessarily. Already Franz was revving the engine insanely to drag the last bit of speed from Lili. Heinz fired the machine gun wildly, in hopes of distracting the enemy. Lili plunged and rolled on the rubble-filled street like a ship in a storm at sea. It made aiming the cannon difficult, but the 75 mm shells from Lili's short-barrelled gun could damage a T-34 only if they made a lucky hit on one of its few weak spots. The sloping armor on the front of the turret was not one.

Despite the violent rocking, Gottfried stuck to his task. Without a specific order from Conrad, he fired. It was a remarkable shot. Few gunners could have hit the T-34's turret from a lurching tank at full speed. Gottfried did. Unfortunately, the shell bounced harmlessly off the armor plate and exploded off to the left.

Erich leaped forward to reload. The T-34's cannon was level now, and the turret was slowly rotating to bring Lili to bear. Conrad knew the Russian shell would not bounce off Lili. At best, it would disable her tracks; some of the crew might have a chance to escape. At worst, it would penetrate the side armor and turn her into a steel coffin. Conrad had seen what was left of a crew after a shell had exploded inside their tank. It had not been possible to know there had been five men in it.

"Come on! Come on!" Conrad urged, as Lili approached the safety of the next corner.

"All right!" Erich yelled.

Gottfried fired.

The shot exploded in front of the T-34, but the dust and rubble thrown up were enough to upset the Russian gunner. His shell exploded behind Lili as she careered behind the safety of the wall.

"Keep going!" Conrad yelled, an idea forming in his mind.

"We can't desert the infantry!" Heinz screamed. "They'll be slaughtered."

"We won't," Conrad replied.

Hoping that the plan of this part of the city was as regular as the suburbs they had passed through, Conrad ordered Franz to proceed for two blocks. Then he turned Lili up a side street to the right. Praying that the infantrymen back at the intersection were keeping the T-34 occupied and that the tank was not supported by antitank gunners, Conrad and Franz worked Lili slowly through the debris of a small apartment block. A brass bedstead, dining room table, stove and chairs were scattered about. A rusted iron treadle sewing machine sat on a table as if its owner had stopped sewing a moment before.

In front of Lili, a wall stood to halfway up the second floor, its blue-and-white-patterned wallpaper looking oddly incongruous amid the destruction. On the center of the wall, Stalin stared disapprovingly at the intruders out of a crooked frame. If Conrad's calculations were correct, the T-34 was on the other side of that wall.

"Aim for Comrade Stalin!" he yelled at Franz.

"Fire as soon as we are through," he ordered Gottfried.

With a crash, Lili exploded through the wall. Large blocks of masonry again cascaded onto her armor. One piece landed on the turret machine gun, knocking it down and bringing the butt up to deal Heinz a solid blow on the side of the head. But ahead of them, not thirty meters away, lay the T-34. Thankfully, its cannon was still aimed at the original intersection. Behind it, Russian soldiers pointed excitedly at Lili. Gottfried had one shot. If he missed, the T-34 wouldn't.

Gottfried seemed to be taking forever. Conrad could feel the sweat running down his neck, but he knew better than to hurry his gunner. He would be aiming for the base of the T-34's turret, where it joined the body. It was one of the weak spots, but it was a frighteningly small target, even from this close range — centimeters up or down and the shell would bounce off.

Lili's cannon fired. Conrad's heart leaped as the T-34's turret left the tank's body and crashed to one side. In the space left behind, Conrad had a split-second's glimpse of what could have been pieces of the Russian crew, before a ball of flame mercifully obscured his view.

"Great shot!" Conrad yelled as Erich busily reloaded.

As the dust cleared, Conrad noticed Russian soldiers working their way toward them. "Put her in reverse, Franz. Heinz, clear those Ivans away before they get too close. Heinz!"

The turret machine gun remained silent. Conrad shook his radio operator's shoulder. Heinz's head slumped to the side and Conrad noticed the ugly bruise on his cheek where the butt of the machine gun had hit him. Not stopping to discover if Heinz was alive or dead, Conrad pushed him away, grabbed the machine gun's handle and pulled the trigger. Nothing happened. Conrad desperately worked the bolt. Still nothing. The collapsing wall must have damaged it.

Lili was reversing blindly back the way they had come. Franz was firing the second machine gun, but it was fixed in the hull and had a narrow traverse. Conrad peered through the turret slit. The Russians were sticking to the sides of the street, using the rubble for cover. Franz's fire was not reaching them. Conrad could hear small-arms fire pinging harmlessly off Lili's armor. Fortunately, the Russians didn't appear to have any antitank weapons.

"Ivans to the left, twenty degrees," Conrad instructed Gottfried. "Take them out."

Six Russian soldiers disappeared in a shower of dust and debris.

Franz had maneuvered Lili onto the side street. Soon they would be back among the German infantry, who would make short work of the Russian soldiers.

Conrad was about to check on Heinz when he saw a movement out of the the corner of his eye. It was close.

"Swivel left ten degrees."

As the turret rotated, the figure of a Russian soldier swept into view. He was about twenty meters away and crouched over. Conrad saw a thin line of black smoke rise from beside the soldier.

"Petrol bomb!" Conrad shouted, cursing their disabled machine gun. There was no time for Gottfried to bring the cannon to bear or for Franz to swing the tank around so the hull machine gun could aim. There was only one hope.

Grabbing his pistol, Conrad rammed his other palm against the hatch lever above his head. A jolt of pain seared up his arm, but the hatch clanged open. Exposing as little of himself as possible, Conrad peered over the lip. The Russian was on his feet now, facing Lili. Each hand held a vodka bottle with a smoldering oily rag tied round its neck. The man drew back his right arm, ready to throw.

Without taking careful aim, Conrad fired his pistol's entire magazine at the man. All his hurried shots missed, except one: one lucky bullet shattered the bottle in the soldier's raised hand. Instantly, the contents exploded into flame, pouring over the soldier. His gasoline-soaked uniform turned him into a living torch. To Conrad's horror, the man began a stumbling run toward Lili — a pillar of flame with the second bottle held out wide to his left.

Conrad pulled the trigger, but the hammer clicked down on an empty chamber. He could only watch helplessly as the burning man staggered forward and smashed the bottle against Lili's vulnerable rear.

With a scream, the man disappeared beneath Lili's tracks, but he had done his work. Flaming petrol engulfed the back end of the tank. Conrad knew it would also be seeping down through seams and cracks toward Lili's petrol supplies. In seconds, she would become a raging death trap.

"Get out!" he screamed as he dropped back into the turret. Already smoke was coming from the engine at the rear. Franz jammed the engine to a stop and hauled the hull hatch open. He scrambled out, closely followed by Erich.

Gottfried held Heinz under the shoulders.

"He's still alive!" he shouted.

Conrad grabbed Heinz's arms and together they manhandled the limp body out of the hatch. There was no time to be careful — they simply pushed until they felt his body fall off the tank. Already it was becoming uncomfortably hot. Conrad waved Gottfried to the hatch. As the gunner's boots disappeared, Conrad hauled himself out. Sharp metal angles dug into his sides and legs as he rolled to the ground. Gottfried was already hauling Heinz away from Lili. The tank's entire back end was engulfed in flames.

Conrad was vaguely aware of bullets chipping the rubble around them as he helped pull Heinz away. Then Lili exploded.

Conrad heard no noise, but he was thrown violently forward by a hurricane of superheated air that scorched his uniform and hair.

When he came to, Lili was burning fiercely and the sounds of gunfire were very close. They were as good as dead — a stunned tank crew with no weapons, at the mercy of approaching Russians.

Gradually, Conrad realized that the firing was coming from the wrong direction. German soldiers advanced toward him, firing over his head at the retreating Russians.

After a short but savage firefight, the street was secure. Conrad, Gottfried, Franz and Erich sat nursing minor cuts, burns and bruises. Heinz lay to one side, breathing gently. A medic was crouched beside him.

"He'll be all right," the medic said. "Just a knock on the head. Take him back to the aid post. You're no use here now anyway. And thanks for getting that T-34."

Conrad smiled wearily and nodded. He looked back at Lili's blackened and twisted remains. Small red flames still licked over her hull, and the explosion of her ammunition had ripped a jagged hole in her side; the hull was gutted and one track was off. Perhaps the engineers could salvage some parts from her, but Lili would never fight again.

SERGEI

Sergei clutches three cans of meat, a package of powdered eggs and two chocolate bars as he awkwardly negotiates a pile of rubble and tries to keep out of sight. The food makes his balance poor, but he is not going to give up such a treasure. It has taken him three days to get it. Three days since he had glimpsed the silver of a parachuted supply canister nestling underneath a collapsed wall. Three days of digging, hiding, waiting and ignoring his mother's cries to be careful and keep out of trouble. Now he has a decent dinner to take back to her in the cellar.

Sergei has adapted well. He knows the safe routes through the ruins and is not bothered by the gruesome sights he comes across or the smell of death in the air. He knows the best places to watch the enemy soldiers while he waits for a chance to steal food.

He has also noticed something about the enemy soldiers. A few weeks ago they were neat and proud. Now they look like beggars, filthy, gaunt and with a strange unfocused gaze. The strain is telling on them, not least because of the Russian snipers.

The snipers are Sergei's heroes. Like ghosts, they drift through the rubble, bringing unexpected death and then vanishing. They are recognizable by their camouflaged clothes and scoped rifles; and they always travel in pairs. When he is old enough, Sergei will be a sniper. Then he will kill a Fascist to pay back mad Tolstoy for the stolen turnip.

Sergei is so engrossed in his dreams of being a sniper that he doesn't hear the bomb. The unexpected blast hurls him painfully forward against a wall.

As his stunned senses return, he checks for his treasure. One can is missing and the powdered eggs are scattered over the surrounding bricks, but he has saved the rest. That is good.

Then Sergei tries to move. He can't. A large block of masonry has slipped from the wall and pinned his left leg painfully to the ground. It is far too heavy to move.

The pain isn't too bad if Sergei stays still, but the cold begins to seep into his small body. He won't last long.

The soldiers find Sergei shivering uncontrollably and drifting in and out of consciousness but still clutching his booty. While they work to free him, Sergei is aware that the soldiers are busy and that one has a shock of red hair, but little else.

After half an hour, he feels his leg pull free. He won't die today.

He stands shakily. His leg hurts, but nothing seems broken. Hiding the cans of meat and the chocolate bars under his coat, Sergei limps away. It is only when he turns to wave thanks and the soldiers wave cheerfully back, that he realizes that the one with red hair is an officer — a German officer.

VASILY

As the dawn light began to suffuse the dust-filled air swirling through the workshops of the Red October Factory, a strange silence fell over the exhausted soldiers huddled behind piles of bricks, ruined walls and abandoned pieces of machinery. It had been a night of disorienting confusion. Small, brutal, isolated battles had erupted without warning, and most of the workshop floor had changed hands at least twice.

As far as Vasily could remember, this was his third dawn in this factory. It was not the factory he had come ashore to six weeks earlier, but that hardly mattered — they were all the same. Living in them was the same and dying in them was the same —Vasily was just glad to be alive another day.

Vasily had not seen Nikolai for hours. Apart from himself and Yelena, Nikolai was the only survivor from the original squad. The other man who had lived through the river crossing had disappeared in a bombing attack.

Vasily's job these past weeks had been to follow Yelena and do exactly what she said. Mostly that had involved crawling a few meters away from her and firing into the darkness to draw German fire so Yelena could spot the enemy muzzle flashes. It was terrifying work, not least because the buildings they fought in held hundreds of bodies, German and Russian; and it was impossible not to crawl over them or lie beside them. But Yelena had taught him the value of the bodies.

"They are good cover," she had whispered one night. "If you're on your own, you stand out. If you are among five or six obviously dead bodies, the Germans will likely assume you are dead too."

Once, Vasily had been cut off by a German squad working around behind him. For almost an hour, he had lain among a pile of cold bodies, inhaling the smell of death and listening to German being whispered a meter or two away until he could crawl back to find Yelena.

During the previous weeks, Yelena had also taught Vasily the sniper's most valuable skill. "Keep moving. Never stay after you have given your position away. When I send you off to distract the Germans, I will fire two or three shots — never more. When you hear them, you will know I am moving and you must too. Move backward and to the side where you last saw me. I will find you and we will go to another location."

This was the pattern they had established in the red-brick building on their first night in Stalingrad, and it had been repeated countless times since in ruined factories, department stores and apartments. Through it all, Vasily rarely had any sense of where he was in relation to the city as a whole. His life was limited to a small area of ruin or a view of a section of street or square through a shell hole or window. The best he could hope for was some sense of their proximity to the river.

Yelena, on the other hand, seemed to have an uncanny sense of direction and could lead them unerringly from a battle in a factory back to a relatively secure cellar where they could snatch some hot food and a few hours' rest.

The pair tried to keep in contact with Nikolai, but Yelena preferred to ply her deadly trade in the lulls in the battles, when targets were easier to distinguish; sometimes they became caught up in larger engagements. Vasily hated those times. There was something clinical and efficient about sniping, but these battles were just a bloody chaos.

A few hours earlier, he and Yelena had been on the second floor. Yelena had wanted to sight through a window on the German side of the building, and Vasily was sent to an adjacent room to provide distracting fire. As he crawled over the rubble toward the window, through which he could see arcing tracer bullets and flares, he heard the click of a rifle bolt. Instinctively, he rolled to one side. A bullet crashed into the wall above his head at the instant Vasily's finger tightened on the trigger, emptying his magazine at the point where he had seen the muzzle flash.

Vasily waited in silence until a flare illuminated the room. In the corner lay a crumpled body, its chest a pulpy mess where the burst of automatic fire had caught it. The corpse's head lolled to one side, but the face was untouched. It was that of a boy not much older than Vasily, and it still wore a look of surprise. The body was dressed in the brown uniform of a Russian rifleman. The boy had fired first. "Stupid!" Vasily said under his breath, as the flare died and the room returned to darkness.

If you had told Vasily a few weeks earlier that he would kill a boy on his own side, he would have been horrified. Now his senses were so finely tuned to pick up the slightest sound that might mean the difference between life and death that there was little room left for common emotion. What did bother him about the incident was that after it, Yelena, who had no way of knowing if he was alive, dead or wounded, had not come to help him. Rationally, he knew she had done the right thing: her presence in the darkened room would only have increased the risk of something else going wrong, but Vasily felt disappointed. He would have gone to help Yelena, whether it was the sensible thing to do or not.

As the daylight strengthened, he was able to make out more of the building around him. While the upper two floors were divided into rooms of varying sizes, the ground level was a vast open workshop. Large pieces of machinery lay thrown about as if scattered by an angry giant. Piles of bricks, some from the ragged holes in the walls, some from the upper levels, had turned the floor into an irregular wasteland. Wide corrugated pipes from an overhead heating system had collapsed and lay like bloated worms. In some places the debris had been arranged to form rough breastworks around which small, vicious battles had raged in the night. Bodies lay everywhere, and the workshop also contained dozens of living soldiers, German and Russian, hidden from the daylight behind the machinery and rubble.

Vasily and Yelena were lying side by side close to the river-side wall of the factory, protected by the concrete base of a machine that had been blown several meters to one side. Yelena lay on her stomach, peering through the scope of her rifle, Vasily on his back with his eyes closed. Sharp fragments of debris dug into his shoulders, but he did not have the will to move. He was little more than an exhausted automaton who did what Yelena told him, and what he had to do to stay alive in the rubble and death. Anything else was a dream.

"So, they haven't killed you yet." Vasily turned his head to see Nikolai crawling toward him. Two new recruits were behind him, awkwardly dragging the heavy machine gun.

"Set it up over there, behind that pile of bricks," Nikolai ordered. "Keep it out of sight but ready to push up into position when the Fascists attack." Turning to Yelena, he asked, "How many Fascists did our sniper get last night?"

Yelena shrugged but didn't take her eyes from her gun sight.

"The Fascists will attack again," Nikolai said. "We

must hold on. Another battalion is being sent in to strengthen us. We must still have a foothold in the factory when they get here."

Vasily craned his neck to look through a shell hole in the wall at the body-strewn wasteland between the factory and the riverbank. It was full daylight now. Any attackers would be slaughtered by the German machine gunners on the floor above.

Almost on cue, a whistle sounded and scores of figures rose from cover and ran forward. At once the heavy throb of machine guns began from above. Soldiers fell, some pirouetting dramatically, others slumping almost apologetically. Vasily watched as one soldier faltered and turned to retreat. The officer behind him shot him in the chest. Almost immediately, a burst of machine gun fire caught the officer. It was insanity, but Vasily had no time to dwell on it. Yelena's rifle cracked three times in quick succession. Vasily slithered up to peer over the concrete. The Germans were attacking through the factory, cunningly darting forward in small groups, using cover, firing as they came.

Yelena fired again and a soldier fell behind some machinery. Vasily fired whenever he saw movement. He was careful to aim well and let off only one shot at a time. He had just one spare magazine left.

To Vasily's left, the squad's machine gun opened fire. The noise reverberated around the factory, deafening those nearby. A German stick grenade whirled through the air and landed in front of Vasily.

He ducked behind the concrete platform as the blast swept over him, peppering him with fragments of brick. Vasily hauled one of his own pineapple-shaped grenades from his belt, pulled out the pin with his teeth and threw it with all his might in the direction the German grenade had come from.

Vasily's grenade was lost in a much louder explosion from the floor above. Fragments of concrete rained down on the soldiers below.

They're shelling the building, Vasily realized. Somehow the Russians had brought a light cannon onto the beach and were shelling the German machine gunners on the floors above.

Behind him, Vasily was aware of a commotion. He glanced back to see the survivors of the attack over the open ground hurl themselves in through doors, windows and ragged holes. They were only a fraction of those who had started out, but they were enough to turn the tide: the German attack, already almost exhausted, collapsed. Russian soldiers sprinted up the stairs to clear the upper floors, firing as they went. Soon most of the building was in Russian hands again, the Germans confined to a few rooms and corners of the workshop. The sounds of battle faded to the softer groans and cries of the wounded.

"Good work," Nikolai said, facing the new recruits. "You two, take the machine gun upstairs so you can fire down on the next German counterattack. The rest of you dig in as well as you can. The screaming vultures will be here soon and we can't expect any reinforcements until dark. We have to hold on our own."

"Come on," Yelena said to Vasily, "We'll go upstairs, too. See what we can get from there. An officer would be good."

Vasily stood up, luxuriating in being upright. Muscles, tensed for hours as he had squeezed himself into the smallest possible space, relaxed.

"So my scout is a sniper's helper now," Nikolai observed. "Well, there's not much use for a scout here. The Fascists aren't hard to find."

Vasily nodded and followed Yelena to the stairs.

On the ruined floor above, Yelena carefully surveyed the scene. Several soldiers manned the windows on the German side of the building. Behind them a doctor tended to some apathetic wounded men. The wall facing the river had several gaping holes. Vasily could see the grove of poplar trees at Krasnaya Sloboda, where he had his first view of Stalingrad almost six weeks earlier. Then he had wondered how people were surviving in the ruins. Now he knew. He also knew how they were dying.

"Here." Vasily turned to see Yelena holding out half a bar of Hershey's chocolate. "I rate American chocolate almost as highly as hand grenades. I doubt any rations will make it through today, so this might be all the food we get."

Vasily felt very weak. His hand was shaking uncontrollably. Suddenly, all the accumulated horrors swept over him. He had learned to hold himself rigidly under control, but in his exhausted state, a beautiful woman offering him a piece of chocolate undid him. Tears poured down his cheeks and he sobbed uncontrollably.

Carefully placing her rifle down, Yelena put her arms around him. Apart from Vasily's heaving shoulders, the pair were immobile, like a sculpture amid the ruins. Gradually his sobbing eased. Yelena relaxed her grip.

"Come on," she said, "eat the chocolate. It will help you feel better."

Vasily wiped his eyes, sniffed loudly and began chewing. Yelena was right, the sweet taste did make him feel better.

"My father thinks American chocolate is decadent," he said at last.

"That may be," Yelena agreed, "but it certainly tastes good."

Vasily had a sudden urge to talk about his father. "He fought in the revolution and thinks everything not Russian is decadent."

"He's one of the Old Guard?"

"Yes. If it wasn't for revolutionaries like him, we'd still be slaves to the czar and wouldn't have everything we have today."

Yelena raised her eyebrows theatrically and looked around at the rubble.

Vasily laughed. "You know what I mean — all the things we are fighting to protect."

"What things?"

Vasily's instinct was to laugh again — everyone knew the benefits of Communism. Yelena's expression was suddenly serious. "Freedom from czarist oppression, for a start."

Yelena nodded. "Comrade Stalin has the ears of an ass," she said loudly.

Horror filled Vasily. In a panic, he looked around to see if anyone had heard. "What are you doing? You'll get us sent to a labor battalion."

Yelena's ironic smile was firmly in place. "It's good that we are free from *czarist* oppression," she said softly.

Before Vasily's confused mind could form a response, the first Stuka of the day began its eerie scream above them.

DAY 160

A VISION OF HELL

Wednesday, November 25, 1942

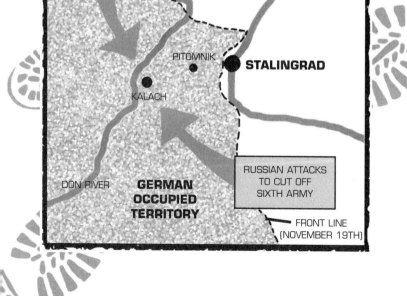

RUSSIAN ATTACKS TO CUT OFF SIXTH ARMY

VOLGA RIVER

PITOMNIK

STALINGRAD

KALACH

RUSSIAN ATTACKS TO CUT OFF SIXTH ARMY

DON RIVER

GERMAN OCCUPIED TERRITORY

FRONT LINE (NOVEMBER 19TH)

0 50 100
KM

CONRAD

"What did they expect, sending us against T-34s in Czech tin cans?" Franz was bitter, and his words spat out in clouds of frosty air. "I could punch a hole through our armor with my fist."

"Save your breath," Conrad said. "You'll need it for walking."

Franz lowered his head into the biting, snow-laden wind and trudged sullenly eastward. Behind Franz, Erich hobbled along, leaning heavily on Heinz's shoulder, his useless right arm strapped to his side with two strips of filthy rag; a bloodstained bandage showed through a long rip in his trouser leg. Since Heinz had been knocked out when Lili had been destroyed, no one had suffered more than odd cuts and bruises — until yesterday. Now Gottfried was dead and Erich was badly hurt and needed a hospital.

All around the crew, men shuffled east, away from the Russians and the column of dark smoke that rose from the burning town of Kalach, where jubilant Russian tank crews embraced each other and celebrated closing the trap on the Sixth Army.

Conrad put his head down and concentrated on walking. He was horribly cold, except for his hands and feet, which had long ago lost all feeling. His black tank uniform did nothing to keep out the cold, and his greatcoat had burned with the tank. At least he had the knitted wool scarf his mother had sent him. Its red color had provoked joking comments about how Conrad had gone over to the Communists. Wrapped around his ears and tucked into his jacket, it did a lot to keep his head warm.

Their situation had deteriorated dramatically in the month since they had lost Lili. First rain had turned the roads to slime that sucked men, vehicles and horses into pits that took hours to escape from. Then the temperature had dropped, the mud had frozen, the rain had turned to snow and the Russians chose to launch their offensive.

If a Panzer division or two with a full complement of tanks and enough fuel had faced the attack, the Russians would not have got very far, but there were no full Panzer divisions. The flanks behind the Sixth Army had been held by poorly equipped Romanian divisions who had stood no chance against the onslaught.

Tankers and soldiers from a dozen units had been cobbled together into a reserve unit, XXXXVIII Panzer Corps, and thrown into the battle to try and stem the tide of T-34s. They had been doomed from the beginning. They had been given light Skoda tanks from

Czechoslovakia, half of which didn't even run. Those that did run, as Franz continually pointed out, were no match for the Russian tanks. The XXXXVIII Corps had been brushed aside in a morning, leaving the steppe dotted with burned-out Skodas.

Conrad and his crew had fought well, but by noon they had run out of petrol and stood, paralyzed, as three T-34s bore down on them. Conrad had ordered everyone out, but only after he had bundled into the snow did he realize that Gottfried had disobeyed to take one last shot at the attackers. It had been a good shot, catching one T-34 in the tracks and disabling it, but two shells had hit back immediately, turning the tank into an inferno that Gottfried had no chance of escaping.

Using the burning tank as cover, the others had run for a treed gully. On the very lip, Erich had been caught in the right shoulder and thigh by a burst of machine-gun fire. Carrying their bleeding friend, Conrad, Heinz and Franz had made it to Kalach, where Erich had been patched up. The Russians had not been far behind, and they had had to head east for Pitomnik, where there was a hospital and an airstrip to fly out the wounded. With luck they would be there before nightfall.

In the gathering darkness, the hospital looked to them as if they had been dropped into hell. Scattered bonfires and oil lanterns provided flickering yellow ponds of light among the deep shadows. Dark figures stumbled and hobbled between the bundles of rags that marked where wounded soldiers lay. The cold air was filled with murmuring, like a low groan of pain.

The hospital itself was in two large buildings that had once been the barns or byres of a collective farm that had escaped destruction in the Russians' retreat. Hundreds of wounded lay outside along the walls. The lucky ones were close to a fire. Unwounded men, too weak to retreat farther, sat stunned or tried to heat up some saved rations or scrounged food. Three exhausted doctors in blood-soaked coats, their faces drawn from lack of sleep, drifted like ghosts, doling out what few medicines they had and changing filthy, lice-ridden dressings.

Conrad led his crew to the nearest doctor, who was working on a boy's face covered in dried blood. Erich was barely conscious and needed to be carried by Heinz and Franz. "We have a wounded man here," Conrad said to the bent form.

The doctor glanced up from his work, his eyes sweeping over Erich's wounds, and pointed toward one of the buildings. "Leave him over by the wall."

Conrad gaped in disbelief. Lines of unconscious, sleeping or dead soldiers lay on the bare ground without even a blanket to keep out the night air. Beside one of the building's doors stood a pile of bodies, higher than a man. Erich wouldn't survive the night there.

"He is wounded in the shoulder and thigh," Conrad persisted. "The wounds need to be cleaned and the dressings changed. There may still be bullets in the wounds."

The doctor shrugged but otherwise ignored them.

Leaving Erich with Heinz, Franz stepped forward, grabbed the doctor by the shoulders and hauled him to his feet. "Our friend is wounded and needs attention." His face was no more than a few centimeters from the doctor's, his unlit cigarette waving with each word.

"What can I do?" the doctor asked tiredly. "There are hundreds of men here. They are all someone's friend. Should I let this boy die to attend to your friend — or anyone else who will probably die anyway? There are too few planes evacuating the wounded, not nearly enough doctors and hardly any medicines."

Franz pulled a pistol out of his belt and prodded the doctor in the stomach. "Finish work on this boy. Then you will work on my friend. You will clean his wounds, change his dressings, give him whatever medicines you have, make him as comfortable as possible and give him an evacuation pass for a plane out tomorrow."

The doctor stared at Franz for a long minute. Then he shrugged again and turned back to the boy on the ground.

After all he had seen, Conrad was still shocked at what Franz had just done. He had threatened an officer — a capital offense. By rights, the military police should be leading Franz away to be executed. But nothing had happened. The world was turning upside down.

After ten minutes of silent work, the doctor stood up. Without so much as a glance at Franz he said, "Bring him this way," and strode toward one of the buildings.

If the yard outside had been hell, Conrad had no name for the threshold he crossed when he entered the building. The air was warmer than outside. In the far corner, a large iron woodstove glowed a dull red. The floor was covered with wounded men who gave the air its distinctive smell, a heavy, sickly scent of carbolic soap, excrement, fear and rot.

The wounded lay on blood-soaked straw, packed like sardines in a can. All were bandaged and many were missing hands, feet, arms or legs. A few close to the door swiveled listless eyes to look at the intruders, but no one moved. Over everything lay a strange silence like a shroud. As if to counter it, the doctor talked as they wound between the bodies toward a table beside the stove. "Frostbite cases are on the rise now that the weather has turned cold. Mostly just fingers and toes, but if we don't get proper winter uniforms it'll soon be hands and feet, then arms and legs.

"Of course, there are also a lot of wounds from this offensive. Most are head or limb wounds. Stomach wounds kill them before they get here.

"Now that the Ivans have cut us off, the only way for the wounded to get out is by plane. We get three or four times as many cases arriving every day as can be flown out. Mind you, the high death rate helps.

"Lift him up." They had reached the table and the doctor shooed away some men who had been sitting on it. Conrad tried not to look too closely as the doctor probed Erich's wounds. When he removed the thigh dressing, Franz and Heinz had to hold their friend down while the doctor dug out a bullet from the muscle. Luckily, Erich soon passed out from the pain.

The doctor bandaged Erich's wounds and filled out a green cardboard tag with Erich's personal information and a brief description of the injuries. Then he signed the card and placed it around Erich's neck.

"Find a place for him till morning," the doctor instructed. "As soon as you hear the first plane approach, get him outside and try to get him aboard. Good luck."

Conrad could find nowhere for Erich in the building but managed to negotiate a place close to one of the courtyard fires in exchange for a promise to keep the fire going through the night. Franz and Heinz went off to scrounge wood, and Conrad settled in by Erich.

Conrad could hardly believe how quickly things had changed. Only weeks ago, the Russians had been on the run, the campaign almost over. Now Lili's crew was decimated and the Sixth Army was besieged. The hopes of the summer had vanished as quickly as the yellow fields of sunflowers they had driven through. Now they were freezing in a desolate world of black and white.

Conrad had no doubt that everything would ultimately work out all right. In a few days they would break out, probably in conjunction with an armored thrust from the west. They would probably have to winter on the Don River, where they had started in August. That wouldn't be too bad, and next summer they could do the job properly. Conrad was certain the soldiers from Stalingrad would be first in line for leave — they certainly deserved it. It would be good to go home and see Mother; she would be very worried despite the cheerful tone Conrad tried to keep in his letters.

And what about Josef? Last Conrad had heard, his brother had been involved in the difficult fighting south of Stalingrad, but some of Hoth's tanks had been caught to the west of the Russian offensive. Conrad could only hope Josef was among them.

Franz and Heinz returned with some broken furniture for the fire. They had also found a loaf of black bread, which the three shared.

"I could use some Hershey chocolate now," Heinz wished dreamily.

"Maybe Hitler took the tanks we didn't get and invaded America with them," Franz speculated. "The great general has probably finished off the Yanks by now and the tanks are on their way back, loaded with Hershey chocolate."

"That's not funny," Heinz said.

"You're right, it's not funny. What is funny is sitting around this fire in the middle of nowhere, eating black bread and wishing for chocolate while Hitler, Goering and the rest live it up in Berlin."

"That's not fair. It's not the Führer's fault."

"Sorry, I forgot." Franz's voice was dripping with sarcasm. "Nothing is the Führer's fault. It's mine for not driving fast enough; or Erich's for not loading fast enough, or Gottfried's for not shooting accurately enough."

At the mention of their dead friend, the group fell silent. Since Gottfried had died, Franz had taken over taunting Heinz about his Nazi fanaticism. Only weeks ago, Conrad would have intervened to stop the baiting. Now he just didn't care. Whoever was to blame was irrelevant. Here they were and they would simply have to make the best of it.

When the bread was gone, Heinz and Franz settled beside Erich and fell asleep. Conrad was afraid he would drop off and let the fire go out, but as exhausted as his body was, his mind was racing. All the fighting to date whirled around, mixed up with worries and speculation about what was going to happen. Eventually, he wrote one of his comforting letters to his mother:

November 26, 1942

Dearest Mother,

This quick note is just to tell you I am well. Erich has been wounded, and we are waiting to load him on the transport out. He will mail this letter from his hospital.

We have had some hard fighting recently but have given a good account of ourselves. We

are all still in splendid spirits, so do not
believe any disturbing rumors you hear. Some
people always look on the negative side. We
have had a setback, there is no denying that,
but it is temporary. The situation will soon be
stabilized and we will be back in control.
When that happens I will try to see Josef. I
do not think we will be home for Christmas
after all, but we will try to spend it together
and drink your health in schnapps.

Thank you for the scarf. I must get some
rest now. I will write more when I can.

Your loving son,
Conrad

Conrad addressed the letter and tucked it into Erich's
jacket. Then he built up the fire and lay back.

The snow had stopped, and the stars glimmered
brightly in the cold darkness. Conrad recognized the
large constellations from wilderness camping in
the Hitler Youth — Ursa Major, Cassiopeia and his
favorite, low on the horizon, the hunter, Orion.
Those had been good days. Days of playing at war.
Conrad chuckled quietly. That's what he had thought
he was doing when Lili had first rumbled east —
playing at war — but the real thing was horribly

uncertain and frightening, and his friends were being maimed and killed.

Conrad shivered and forced himself to think about the breakout and relief. It wouldn't be long now. It would be so good to get back to a relatively secure billet. He took out his father's Iron Cross and held the cold metal in his hand. Had his father thought he was going off on a big adventure when he went off to war in 1914? Probably. Who could have known that the Great War would turn into the horror it had. Maybe boys and young men in every war went off thinking it was a noble adventure — and every generation had to learn in blood that war was only an adventure in the minds of boys who had never fought and old men who didn't have to.

The sky lightened in the east. Conrad had dropped off, but the fire was still glowing and burst into flame when he added the last of the broken furniture. Franz and Heinz melted some dirty snow to make warm tea. Even Erich woke and sipped a little.

"Won't be long now, you lucky sod," Franz said enviously. "Don't seduce all the girls in Berlin. Leave some for the rest of us."

"He won't find any girls. No girl will even look at him," Heinz countered. "They're all waiting for me."

"Don't be so sure," Erich said slowly. "Once I show them my wound, I'll be irresistible. You guys will just have to wait your turn."

The four men laughed.

"I put a letter for my mother in your pocket last night," Conrad said. "Would you mail it for me?"

Erich nodded and felt the letter in his pocket.

"And mine too?" Heinz asked, handing over a folded sheet of paper.

"And this one to the wife?" Franz asked a little sheepishly. "I need more tobacco."

"I'll deliver them," Erich said. "On my way back to the farm."

"Thank you," Franz and Conrad said together.

"Yes, thanks," Heinz added. "Are there any girls on your farm?"

"My daughters," Erich said. "But if I catch you within ten kilometers of either of them, you'll wish you were back fighting the Russians."

The banter was interrupted by a growing restlessness in the crowd. Men were standing and staring to the west. At length, a low droning sound was followed by the sight of a tiny black dot on the horizon. The crowd began to move toward the beaten-snow runway. Those who could dragged themselves along, and the more serious cases were carried or helped by friends. Others just lay where they were and pleaded with those around them for assistance.

"Here comes the first flight," Conrad said. "Keep hold of your pass home. It's going to be quite a scramble to get on board."

Heinz and Franz lifted Erich and followed Conrad as he barged a path through the crowd. By the time they had reached the end of the runway, the plane, a three-engine Junkers 52, had taxied to a stop. The crowd watched in silence as doors in the ribbed fuselage opened and crates and boxes were unloaded onto the snow.

A line of military police, machine pistols at the ready, faced the restless mass: very few of those waiting would fit on the plane, and a discontented murmur ran through the crowd.

"My friend has a pass," Conrad said to the nearest policeman.

The man ignored him.

"My friend is badly wounded," Conrad tried again. "He has a pass to fly out on this plane. Can you let us through?"

The policeman turned his disinterested gaze on Conrad. "Everyone has a pass," he said. "Your friend's no one special."

Behind him, Conrad felt Franz move. He held his hand back to restrain his friend. If he tried the pistol threat on the military police, Conrad had no doubt he would be shot in seconds.

"Give me your name," Conrad ordered as officiously as he could manage.

The policeman hesitated. "Why?"

Conrad detected a hint of uncertainty in the man's voice. He pressed his advantage. "Because I shall take this up with your superiors. Do you know who this man is?"

The policeman shook his head. Conrad held Erich's tag in front of him. The man blanched visibly at the first line: Erich Himmler. Heinrich Himmler's SS controlled a secret-service organization whose tentacles wound through every aspect of German life.

"Is he related?" the policeman asked.

"Wrong question," Conrad said as arrogantly as he could manage. "The right question is whether you can risk that he is. Now, either let my friend through or give me your name, rank and serial number."

The policeman glanced around — there was no help to be seen.

"All right," he grumbled as he let the four past.

At the sight of someone being ushered through the cordon, the crowd surged forward. Conrad heard scattered gunshots, but the police line broke. People surged around Conrad and his crew. "Run!" he yelled.

Some of the fittest in the crowd had reached the plane and were hauling out boxes of supplies and throwing them haphazardly to the ground. Dragging Erich along, the three lashed out with their fists as they forced their way through the mass before the pilot could panic and take off. With a final effort they were beside the door, out of which the last of the cargo was being pushed.

Lightly wounded men were dragging themselves into the plane past the bewildered crew. The more seriously wounded were being lifted in, if they had friends to lift them. The rest simply looked on or begged for help.

With Heinz and Franz's help, Conrad hoisted Erich into the plane. He tried to be careful, but his friend screamed in agony. Conrad climbed in and maneuvered Erich so that he was lying to one side. The floor of the plane was covered with soldiers, many with no visible wound.

"Lie still," Conrad advised. "You'll be in hospital surrounded by pretty nurses before you know it."

A thought occurred to Conrad. He could escape — and he didn't even have to do anything. If he just lay down beside Erich, in less than an hour he would be out — safe, warm, well fed.

The pilot was revving the engines and the crew were struggling to close the door. Conrad could still see the snow swirling above the heads of the desperate men on the runway. This was how Stalingrad would end unless they broke out soon — a disorganized rabble, fighting one another to escape, to survive. Conrad had that chance. All he had to do was keep still and he would be safe.

But he couldn't. Two of that rabble were his friends, his crew, his responsibility. With an immense effort of will, Conrad moved to the door.

"Good luck!" he yelled to Erich as he jumped down into the snow. Behind him the doors clanged shut and the plane began to move. The propellors raised a cloud of snow as it gathered speed and lifted into the morning sky. With a low sigh, the crowd shuffled back to the hospital to await the next plane, ignoring the scattered men who had been trampled in the stampede.

"You could have gone," Franz said quietly.

"No," Conrad replied, "I couldn't. Anyway, what would you two hopeless cases do without me to give you orders.

"Word is that Streicher is forming a battle group to try to stabilize the line. We might as well lend a hand there."

Silently, the three trudged through the snow toward the distant sounds of battle.

SERGEI

Sergei is cutting off the end of a sausage where the dead German's blood has soaked into it. The rest of it is edible and will make a fine meal to celebrate the good news sweeping through the ruined city like smoke — the great counterattack has begun. Now it is the German armies who are trapped.

Talk and laughter fill the crowded basement where a dozen families from Sergei's destroyed apartment block live. The air in the poorly ventilated room is heavy with the smell of unwashed bodies and cooked food, and faces are pale from fear and lack of sunlight. Some nights the temperature drops to twenty degrees below zero, but tonight everyone is cheerful.

Sergei chews contentedly. His mother still nags him to be careful, but each time he returns from one of his forays with a hunk of bread or a piece of sausage, her words have a little less conviction. Even Tolstoy holds no fear for him anymore. Sergei knows his way around the ruined city as well as he *knew his own bedroom before it was bombed.*

Sergei swallows the sausage and looks up. A silence is creeping across the chatter-filled room like a blanket.

The entrance to the cellar is an irregular hole in the wall that leads to a dank passage sloping upward to emerge near Tolstoy's allotment. The hole is so low that adults have to duck to enter and exit. Now it is blocked by Tolstoy's hunched shape. He is waving a rifle about wildly and scanning the room.

"Put the rifle down, old man!" someone shouts. "You're more dangerous than the Germans."

Tolstoy ignores the comment and the following laughter. He makes his way over to Sergei and thrusts the rifle at him.

"Have you paid for your turnip yet?" he asks, his eyes wild.
"No."

"Here! Take this rifle. Do it. Kill the invader of our sacred homeland. Kill the one who has raped our women, murdered our men and destroyed our city."

Sergei cringes back from the old man. His mother moves forward.

"Get away from my son," she orders. "I don't want any trouble."

"Cowards!" Tolstoy spits. He shoves the rifle at Sergei and stumbles across the room, mumbling incoherently.

"Madman," Sergei's mother says. "Take that rifle outside and throw it away. If the Germans find weapons in here, they'll kill us all."

Sergei picks up the weapon — it is surprisingly heavy — and makes his way over to the entrance. It would be a shame to lose the rifle. His mother is right, they can't keep it in the cellar, but Sergei knows plenty of hiding places. Then he can take it with him on his expeditions. He can be a sniper.

Sergei has pictures of famous snipers under his mattress on the cellar floor — Zaitsev, Zikan, Chekov and the others. His favorite is Yelena Pavlova. He updates her score — forty-two at last count — every time a news sheet is circulated. He even saw her once, a lithe shadow stepping through the ruins.

Sergei works his way over to a large rusted water tank. Carefully, he slips the rifle behind it and piles stones over it. Satisfied that it is well hidden, he returns to the cellar. He's happy. With a bit of practice, he will be a sniper, just like Pavlova.

VASILY

Very slowly, Vasily raised his helmet above the window ledge. The bullet split the metal along the right side and sent the helmet spinning across the room. At the next window, Yelena's rifle barked.

"Did you get him?" Vasily asked as he put down the stick his helmet had been balanced on.

"Of course. Do I ever miss?"

"Well," Vasily said. "There was that fat sergeant last week. He was such a big target that even I could have hit him."

"Not with a bomb exploding in your lap."

"It was at least ten meters away. And what about the officer the week before."

"All right. So I'm not perfect. How many Germans have you killed?"

"Five or six, as far as I can tell, and I know what you're going to say next. That this one who just ruined another helmet takes your score to forty-three. That leaves only about two hundred and fifty thousand to take care of."

Yelena laughed, her eyes sparkling beneath the fur trim of her hat. The cold weather of the past few days mercifully masked the pervasive smell of death, and the first heavy snowfall had hidden much of the destruction. But these were small benefits. In the past month, the remnants of the 13th Guards and the rest of 62nd Army had been relentlessly pushed back. Now they held only three tiny bridgeheads in the city, none deeper than a thousand meters, and already the ice was sweeping down the river, cutting off communications with the east bank. Until it froze solid enough to carry vehicles, their only supplies would come from the air force, which could drop only at night and frequently missed the bridgeheads. What had really kept them going was the persistent rumor that a big offensive was being prepared to attack the Germans in the rear. Now, far to the west, the attack was under way.

"We'd better get back to the bunker," Yelena said, rolling back from the window. "It'll be too dark to shoot by the time we take a new position, and even the Germans aren't stupid enough to keep showing themselves here. I'm not going to get my officer today. Besides, someone is supposed to be coming to interview me for one of those propaganda sheets."

"You're famous."

Yelena laughed. "Only because the commissars need heroes. I just wish they would get it right. I tell them one thing and it appears as something completely different. The person they write about is nothing like me. The last one had me shooting wolves in the forest when I was five years old. I've never seen a wolf. Now, rats — there's something I know about."

An hour later, Vasily and Yelena were sitting in plush, matching armchairs in their bunker, clutching tin mugs of hot tea. The bunker had been the cellar of a luxurious apartment block for high Communist Party officials. It stood on the Volga bank, commanding superb views over the river. Once eight stories high, its white walls had been a landmark for the river traffic. German bombs and shells had reduced the walls to skeletal ruins and filled the interior with rubble, broken furniture and personal possessions.

Back in August, the cellar had been used as an air-raid shelter, and someone had dragged the two armchairs down to make their time there more comfortable. The chairs' owners, along with the other civilian residents, had long since disappeared — dead or evacuated — and the cellar was now filled with soldiers. Early on, Vasily and Yelena had commandeered the chairs and moved them into a corner. No one had tried to take them away because Yelena was a sniper and snipers were revered by the commissars. This corner was an oasis of calm in the bustle of the cellar where Vasily and Yelena ate, slept and talked.

They rarely talked about the war or the present. Vasily told Yelena about life in Moscow and repeated his father's stories about the revolution in Petrograd. Occasionally, Yelena told a tale of the farmers she had grown up among in the foothills of the Ural Mountains, but mostly she was content to listen to Vasily's stories, that enigmatic smile playing on her lips. Tonight was different. The cellar was abuzz with the great news. The attack that would crush the Fascist invaders and relieve the beleaguered fighters in Stalingrad was going better than anyone had hoped. Mighty tank armies were smashing through the weak flanks covering the German Sixth Army's rear, sweeping across the snow-covered steppe from north and south to join up at the pivotal town of Kalach.

"Nothing can stop them," Vasily said gleefully. "Once our armies meet at Kalach, the Fascists will be caught like rats in a trap."

"Yes," Yelena replied, "but rats, especially trapped ones, can give you a nasty bite."

"Do you think they will try to break out?"

"That would be the sensible thing to do."

"Yes," Vasily agreed. "They will concentrate and try to break out to the west. The battle of Stalingrad is almost over."

Vasily was distracted by someone across the cellar playing a catchy tune on an old accordion. Suddenly, the room was transformed into a dance hall. Filthy, unshaven soldiers cavorted like children, flinging their arms and legs wide in imitation of Cossack dances. Bottles of vodka were passed around and drained with abandon.

"It would be the sensible thing to do." Yelena pulled Vasily back to their conversation. "But will Hitler do the sensible thing? This is not a rational battle. First Hitler ordered his tanks into the streets of the city, where they lost all advantage and we could pick off their soldiers at will. Snipers don't do well on the open steppe.

"Then we were ordered to fight for every room in the city — not one step backward — when the sensible thing would have been to withdraw across the river and pound the Germans with artillery and bombers."

"Are you equating Comrade Stalin's decisions with Hitler's?" Vasily was getting used to Yelena's questioning, but saying Comrade Stalin and Hitler were the same was going too far.

"I am certain Comrade Stalin had it planned down to the last detail." Yelena's tone was serious, but it was undermined by her ironic smile. "Not a single soldier has died needlessly in Stalingrad."

"But we have to fight them to the finish," Vasily protested.

"I agree. It's the way the fight is organized that I question. And that's important — I question. Back at Kamyshin I could have been shot for that. Here, soldiers complain, make jokes about Stalin, sing subversive songs — and there is nothing the commissars can do. Maybe change will come out of this war."

"Why do we need change? Hasn't Comrade Stalin performed wonders? The five-year plans. The collective farms. What about the great industrial projects and the railway through Siberia? These are continuing the revolution."

"The Socialist Paradise," Yelena said bitterly.

"Not yet!" Vasily felt anger rising. "But steps toward it."

Yelena gazed intently at Vasily's face. Then she leaned forward and spoke softly. "You were protected in the city, but think. Do you know of anyone who disappeared?"

"Disappeared?"

"Yes. Just vanished. Or perhaps went away for re-education and never returned?"

An old memory flickered in Vasily's mind. His brow furrowed with the effort of dredging it up. "There was Uncle Aleksandr. He used to visit us in the apartment when I was little — eight or nine. He wasn't a relative but a friend of father's from the old days, so I called him 'uncle.' He had been an important revolutionary — even met Comrade Lenin. He had a huge mustache, even bigger than Comrade Stalin's, and he used to sit me on his knee and tell me stories from the civil war, of cavalry charges across the steppe to defeat the Whites and the foreigners trying to bring back the czars."

"Did he ever talk about Comrade Trotsky?"

Vasily cringed at the name of the man who had been Lenin's friend. Vasily's father said he had tried to undermine the revolution. "Yes. Uncle Aleksandr said that Trotsky was a brilliant soldier, and he was the reason the Red Army won the civil war. But that was before anyone knew that he was trying to betray the revolution."

Yelena nodded encouragement. "And what happened to Uncle Aleksandr?"

"He … disappeared," Vasily said quietly. "He just stopped coming round. I missed him. I asked Father where he was. He said that he had been denounced as a counterrevolutionary and had been sent for reeducation. He said it was a good thing and that Uncle Aleksandr would come back a better person, but he looked sad — and Uncle Aleksandr never came back."

"What happened to him?"

"I don't know."

"I do. One of two things. Either he was taken to the Lubyanka Prison, where he was probably tortured to name other 'counterrevolutionaries.' Then, when he had told them everything he knew, he was ordered to the cellar. As he went down the stairs, the guard behind him would have shot him in the base of the skull. He would have been dead before he hit the floor.

"If that happened, he was lucky. If he was unlucky, he was sent to one of the camps. There he might have lived for several years, building a hydroelectric dam or working on that railway you are so proud of. Then he would have died of cold or starvation or a beating."

Vasily stared wide-eyed. The accordion music seemed to be from another world. "How do you know this?"

Yelena stared back, her eyes hard and dark. "Because it happened to my father."

"Your father was a counterrevolutionary?" The words spilled out of Vasily before he could stop them.

"No," Yelena said, her smile wintry. "My father was a farmer. A good one. He worked to make his farm produce as much as possible. He wrote away for new seeds so he could find out which crops did best. He took care of the soil, fertilizing it and letting it lie fallow when it needed that. He used the latest scientific techniques and the latest equipment. The yield of his fields doubled and tripled. With the extra income, he bought up patches of land abandoned when a family died or moved away. Soon he was the most successful farmer for many kilometers around."

"He did well, then."

"Yes, but he made a lot of enemies. The other peasants resented his success, even though he tried to share it. He offered them new seeds and taught different ways of caring for their fields. But it was no good. They couldn't or wouldn't change the way things had been done for generations. That's the trouble with Russia — no one ever wants to change. That's why we have revolutions.

"Anyway, when I was a child, someone in the village denounced my father to the local Soviet. They said he was a Kulak — a landowner who profited while those around him starved — a capitalist who had never embraced the revolution.

"The day they took him away, two men in black leather coats and city shoes came. Father explained how he had tried to improve everyone's lot, but they put him in a big car and drove off.

"Mother always said he would come back. She never gave up. For years, she wrote letters — to Comrade Stalin himself. When she never got a reply she went all the way to Moscow to badger officials into releasing my father. All it did was kill my mother. She came back a bitter, broken woman. It was she who told me about Lubyanka and the camps. Where she found out, I have no idea, but I do not doubt her; she talked with such desolate intensity.

"She died when I was eleven. The farm had been split up among the peasants who had denounced Father. You see, unlike your story of the farmer and the bear, in my village, the farmer didn't trick the bear. The bear won.

"Anyway, I went back to living with the uncle who had looked after me while Mother was away. He was a strange old man, a recluse who lived in the forest. He hunted and trapped to survive. He taught me to shoot. His only luxury was a library. As a child I thought he must have every book ever written and I was determined to read every one. I didn't, but I read most of them, some several times.

"So I can do two things very well. I can discuss Dostoevsky with a university professor, and I can shoot a man through the eye at five hundred meters."

Was it true? Vasily's instinct was to say it was. Over the past few weeks, he had fallen into the habit of doing exactly what Yelena said, and it had saved his life several times. She would never lie to him.

But if what she said was true — if honest, decent people like Uncle Aleksandr and Yelena's father were just taken away and killed … or worse — what was he fighting for? Wouldn't that make Stalin's Russia as bad as Hitler's Germany?

No! Vasily couldn't accept that. Russia was worth fighting for to the last drop of his blood. Under Comrade Stalin, Russia had modernized and thrown off the shackles of czardom and serfdom — of slavery. It was a modern country now, a great country. Yelena wouldn't lie to him, so she must be mistaken.

"You're wrong," he said angrily. "It must —"

"Whoosh wrong?"

Vasily turned at the slurred interruption to see Nikolai standing behind him. He held a half-empty vodka bottle in his right hand and his cartridge lighter in his left. He was having trouble standing upright. How long had he been there?

"I'll tell you whoosh wrong," Nikolai went on. "Hitlersh wrong. Thatsh who. Wrong to come here 'n' wrong to think any German sholdier'll be left alive 'fter thish battlsh over. We've gott'm 'n the run. Com'n have a drink. Shelebrate. I've gotta preshent for you."

Nikolai grabbed Vasily by the arm and dragged him to his feet. He thrust the vodka bottle at him.

"Drink," he said.

Vasily took a sip. The harsh liquid burned his throat.

"Good boy," Nikolai said. "That one'sh for Yevgeny — 'member Yevgeny?" Nikolai let out an impressive belch. "Now have one for th'ol' squad. Good ol' squad. We've got a lot of ol' comradsh to drink to. Lot of dead men to drink to. Then we can dance. And thish's for you."

Nikolai clumsily thrust his lighter into Vasily's hand. "I want you to have it."

"But, your lighter …" Vasily began, thinking of the countless times he had seen Nikolai compulsively flicking it when he was under stress.

"Vashily," Nikolai said thickly, "you're a good boy. I like you. Thish's my wedding preshent to you."

"But —" Getting married?

Nikolai grabbed his arm and dragged him in a zigzag course across the room. Helplessly, Vasily looked back at Yelena. Her ironic smile was in place.

DAYS 189-190

CHRISTMAS

Thursday–Friday,
December 24–25, 1942

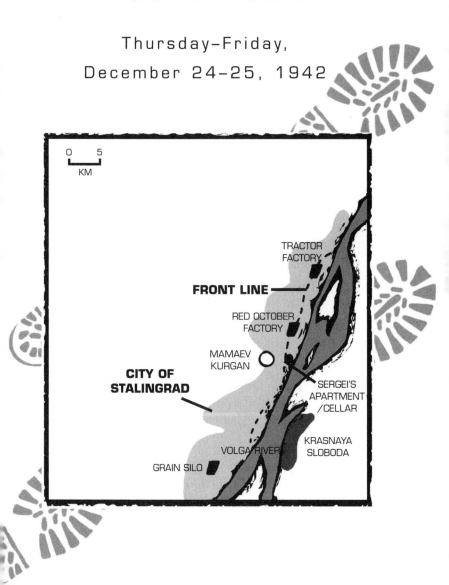

CONRAD

Conrad trudged on into the biting wind. He could no longer feel his feet but knew he was walking by the painful shudder that passed up his legs with each step. Most of the time he kept his eyes closed. When he did force them open, all he saw was the patch of windblown snow immediately in front of him, the monotony broken occasionally by frozen, blackened limbs sticking out of the white.

"Once we get back into Stalingrad," Heinz whispered into Conrad's left ear, "we can warm up and then break out to meet Hoth's attack."

"Hoth's not coming back," Gottfried said, on Conrad's right. "It's been a week since we could hear his guns. That was our chance to break out. Hoth couldn't have been more than fifty kilometers away. But what did your precious Hitler say? Stay and fight. Don't give up a centimeter of conquered soil. We've been retreating steadily since then. Hoth must be two hundred kilometers away by now."

"If we had a damned tank," Franz growled, "then we could do something. We're tank men, but all they can give us to stop the whole damned Russian army is a rifle and a few grenades."

"Things will turn around. The Führer has a plan, you'll see." Conrad was amazed at Heinz's blind optimism — no setback could make a dent in it.

"The Führer! Stalin!" Erich spat. "Power-crazed maniacs who want to rule the world. And who pays? Poor slobs like us. The only plan the Führer has is to let us die here in this godforsaken place."

"If only we had a tank," Franz said.

Conrad was astonished that his friends had the energy to argue when it was all he could do to keep walking. And he was better off than they were. He had winter boots and a quilted jacket taken from a Russian corpse. He had discarded his helmet long ago and instead wore the thick, knitted scarf his mother had sent him.

Franz was the worst off. He had lost his greatcoat and his feet were wrapped in rags. They were in terrible shape — black and frozen solid. One of his toes had broken off like a piece of dead wood. No wonder Franz had collapsed beside the road, dead before Conrad could stumble over to him.

Wait — that couldn't be right. Conrad's sluggish brain fought to understand. If Franz had died beside the road, how could he be talking to Conrad now? And Erich — Erich had got out on the plane. And Gottfried had died, screaming in a burning tank.

With an immense effort, Conrad lifted his head and squinted around him. He was alone. Despair overwhelmed him.

He must have fallen asleep while walking and dreamed the others were talking to him. But they were all dead, even Heinz. Conrad slumped into a snowbank piled against a ruined wall. It was too much — too much death. Heinz had been the worst. Just yesterday he really had been walking beside Conrad.

The fighting out on the steppe had been hopeless — starving, frozen men scratching holes in the rock-hard earth to try to stop Russian tanks. Eventually it had all fallen apart, and the survivors had headed toward the false security of the city.

During the retreat, Conrad had seen roadsides cluttered with frozen corpses and those who could walk no farther. When a rare horse-drawn cart passed, a groan would rise from the pitiful bundles of rags, and the fittest would struggle forward to beg a ride. Only capable of incoherent grunts, they would totter on frozen, unbending legs, waving sticklike arms and blackened hands missing fingers that had snapped off in the cold. Conrad never saw a cart stop.

Conrad and Heinz had tried to keep to the center of the crowd so that they were protected from the wind, but yesterday, as they approached Stalingrad's suburbs, they had been almost alone.

"Hoth will attack again." Heinz had said. "All we in the *Kessel* have to do is hold on until then."

The very fact that Stalingrad had become a *Kessel* — a fortress — meant that the campaign had failed. Besides, a fortress couldn't hold out without supplies, and very few were getting through on the planes.

Conrad was debating with himself whether to waste his energy arguing with Heinz when the shell landed. The blast stunned Conrad and threw him to one side. A piece of shrapnel gouged a long cut in his left arm.

The first thing he saw when he came to was one of Heinz's legs in the snow beside him. The other was still attached to Heinz's body by a few tendons and scraps of flesh.

Conrad cradled his companion's head and talked to him till the end. The shock and cold deadened the pain and Heinz died peacefully. His last words had been a joke about how his injury would provoke the sympathy of all the pretty girls back home.

Leaving Heinz had been the hardest thing Conrad had ever done. What was the point of going on? Why was he alive when everyone else was dead? The only thing that got him moving again had been the hope that Josef might still be fighting in Stalingrad. A straggler had told him that Josef was not with Hoth's relieving column but had been cut off in the city. It was a slim hope, but it had been justified. Just that morning soldiers had told him not only that Josef was still alive but also where he was.

Conrad hauled himself painfully out of the snowbank and staggered on. Half an hour later, he fell down the steps into a command bunker under a ruined house only a kilometer from the Volga.

The command post measured about five meters square, but the wooden beams supporting the roof forced everyone to crouch. One wall was taken up with a low cot and a squat stove. Opposite the entrance, a table supported the black bulk of a radio, covered in dials and sprouting wires and plugs. The radio operator turned to look at Conrad.

Opposite the cot was a desk, its surface almost covered with overlapping maps and papers held in place by a Luger pistol. An infantryman's helmet and several other pieces of equipment hung from nails pounded into the roof beams. Rivulets of water trickled down the walls and pooled on the floor. Light was provided by a sputtering oil lamp hanging above the desk and a candle sitting on the handle of a bayonet wedged into a crack in the wall at the head of the cot. What little space was left was occupied by *Oberst* Josef Zeitsler, staring openmouthed at his guest.

"Conrad?" he asked, as his brother picked himself up.

Conrad nodded. "Josef."

Josef embraced his brother. "Where have you come from? How did you get here?"

Conrad made no attempt to answer Josef's flurry of questions. It was enough just to clumsily return his embrace. He was happy. He wasn't responsible for men's lives any more. He wasn't a tank commander, just a little brother. Josef would make everything right.

And it was warm. A Berliner would consider it bitterly cold, but Conrad was warmer than he could ever remember. His cheeks tingled and sweat prickled his skin. Needles of exquisite pain lanced through his hands and feet as the numbness retreated.

Josef held Conrad at arm's length and scrutinized his face. "You look dreadful."

Conrad smiled weakly. "I'm hungry."

"Of course." Josef turned to the radio operator. "Heinrich. See if you can find some soup and sausage for my brother. I think we have saved some for our Christmas feast."

As Heinrich squeezed past, Conrad was amazed at how plump and well fed the man looked — he hadn't seen anyone that healthy for ages. There was color in his face and his features looked rounded and smooth, a far cry from the faces Conrad was used to: shocked with sunken eyes staring out from angular skulls covered with stretched, gray skin. Obviously, officers in the city were eating better than the men out on the steppe.

"You are an *Oberst* now," Conrad said, noticing Josef's uniform. "Quite a promotion."

"Yes." Josef laughed bitterly. "I am a mighty *Oberst*. In charge of an entire regiment. Trouble is, there is hardly any regiment left and our last tank ran out of fuel days ago. We have precious little ammunition, quarter rations of food and whatever winter clothing we can take from dead Ivans. Promotions are thick in the air these days.

"Take off your coat. Sit down." Josef fussed around his brother, helping to remove the Russian jacket that Conrad had opened to reveal his uniform so he wouldn't be shot by a nervous sentry as he approached the bunker.

Josef unwrapped the rags that Conrad had bound around his boots for insulation. He cleaned and redressed the wound in Conrad's arm, sprinkling it with antibiotic powder. It would heal in time; there was no gangrenous tissue and the parasites congregated around it were few. Conrad had seen wounds green with infection and barely visible beneath a seething mass of voracious lice.

Josef examined Conrad's hands and feet with particular care. The fingers and toes were still numb, swollen and a deep red color, but they were black only at the tips. That meant they probably wouldn't have to be amputated. Conrad had seen men whose legs were so black and frozen that they broke if the men tried to run.

As Josef fussed, he kept up a constant chatter that required no response from Conrad apart from an occasional nod.

"I was really worried about you, Conrad. Mother has heard nothing since the letter you sent out with that wounded tank man. I knew things were worse out on the open steppe, but I had no way of contacting you. No one knew where you had got to after the Russian breakthrough.

"But we will spend Christmas together after all, if not quite what we planned in Kharkov. Mother wrote that you kept talking about the family being together. I must send a note out to let her know you are all right."

At length, Conrad was settled to Josef's satisfaction. He was exhausted, malnourished, filthy, lice-ridden and in rags, but he felt wonderful. The radio operator returned with a bowl of steaming soup and a plate of dark sausage and black bread. The soup was mostly water, the sausage gristle and horsemeat and the bread sawdust, but it tasted good.

"Thank you, Heinrich," Josef said. "Go get some rest. I will take any messages that come through."

The operator saluted and left.

Josef guided Conrad to the desk and sat him down. He put the food on the maps in front of him. Clutching the spoon awkwardly in his numb fingers, Conrad began to eat.

"Ow!" he exclaimed as he attempted to bite into the hard bread. "My teeth!"

"When did you last eat fresh food?"

Conrad shrugged helplessly.

"Probably the beginnings of scurvy. Soak the bread in the soup."

Conrad ate in silence. He concentrated on each mouthful as if it were a complex math problem in school. It was all he could do to stop himself plunging his face into the soup and stuffing the bread and sausage until his cheeks bulged, but he focused on one mouthful at a time.

A feeling of warmth and comfort overcame him.

His body relaxed and even the pain in his hands and feet was welcome. Now he could rest without worrying that he would never awake.

Yet the weeks of being alert for the slightest sound of danger kept his brain whirling: the telltale sound of a boot crunching on dry snow or the cough of a hidden sentry had saved his life too many times. Every sound in the dugout, from Josef's voice to the almost inaudible scuttling of a rat in the corner, shouted in Conrad's head. Besides, there was something he had to do — if only he could remember what.

He wiped the last bit of bread around the tin bowl and sucked up the last drop of soup. He sat back, nibbling gently on the sausage.

"Feel better?" Josef asked.

"Yes."

"Do you want to sleep?" Josef indicated the cot.

Conrad gazed at the simple army cot against the wall. When was the last time he had slept in anything like a bed? He couldn't remember. The last time he could recall being comfortable was on a straw bale beneath Lili's friendly hull. Anything before that was too alien to mean anything.

Then he remembered what he had to do. Reaching awkwardly into his pocket, he pulled out his father's Iron Cross.

"Here," he said, handing it to Josef. "I promised to return it. Thank you for the loan." Then he pitched forward into darkness.

The jagged ring of the radio bell dragged Conrad out of sleep. For a long moment he wondered if he was dead, he felt so comfortable and warm. Then he heard Josef's voice and memory slowly returned.

"Be especially vigilant. The Russians know it's Christmas Day and will probably try to take advantage of any sign of relaxation. The cold weather and the snow might discourage them, but we can't be too careful.

"I will make a round of the company headquarters this morning to check dispositions. Even if the Ivans don't attack today, we are due for action soon. Happy Christmas."

The radio clicked off and Conrad opened his eyes.

"Good morning," Josef said with a smile. "It's another beautiful winter day in the *Kessel*. Happy Christmas."

"Happy Christmas. I'm afraid I didn't bring you a present."

"That's okay. I haven't seen a tree to put it under in weeks. How are you feeling?"

Conrad sat up. He seemed remarkably well. Most of the sensation had returned to his extremities and, apart from aching all over, he was better than he had been in quite a while.

"Not bad," he said, standing. "A good night's sleep is a wonderful restorative."

"Good. Have a mug of tea. It's pretty weak but it will help."

Conrad grasped the hot tin mug. He was grateful, but he couldn't restrain an edge of bitterness in his voice. "You have things better here than out on the steppe."

"Yes," Josef replied. "Horsemeat sausage and tea on Christmas Day. But don't assume we live at this high standard all the time. The bread ration is to be halved again tomorrow and there are few horses left. The doctors are beginning to report deaths from malnutrition.

"The thing I hate about city fighting, though, is the lack of space. On the steppe your enemy might be better fed and armed than you, but at least you could see him coming. Here death just happens without warning. If you relax, even for a minute, you're as good as dead.

"Look at this." Josef opened a large sack beside the radio table. About a dozen grenades were tied together with wire. In the middle was a large jam tin. "This passes as sophisticated weaponry these days. Fill the can with steel balls and you have a shrapnel bomb. Fill it with extra explosives, like this one, and you have a bunker destroyer. Crude, and you can't throw them very far, but effective if you can roll them down some steps. There's a soldier in C Company who has become quite expert at destroying strongpoints with these things.

"The *Kessel* is doomed. Hoth hasn't the strength to break in and Hitler has forbidden a breakout. We'll just get weaker and weaker until the Ivans can pick us off at will.

"Last night, before you showed up, a crowd of us were having a drink to toast loved ones back home. Do you know what the conversation turned to?"

Conrad shook his head. He had been expecting his big brother to magically make everything all right.

"Suicide," Josef said bleakly. "It's Christmas Eve and the only thing we can discuss is the best way to kill ourselves. The best the optimist among us could suggest was deserting."

"Deserting to the Russians?"

"No. That would just delay the inevitable. What he suggested was dressing in Russian uniforms, teaming up with those poor Russians fighting on our side and trying to make it through to our lines."

"Our lines must be two hundred kilometers away! It's impossible."

"Yes, but so is staying here."

On some level Conrad had known for some time that the *Kessel* was doomed, but he had been wrapped up in the tiny world of his own survival. To hear his brother say it rationally in the relative comfort of a command bunker brought the enormity of the disaster home. The entire Sixth Army — hundreds of thousands of men — doomed.

"Enough," said Josef. "It seems impossible to have a conversation these days without talking about death. Remember you gave me this last night?" Josef held out the Iron Cross.

"Yes. I want you to have it back."

"Thank you. Last night, I spent a long time thinking. Remember how we used to say that our war was different from Father's? We were wrong. It's just the same. Only the weapons are a bit more efficient." Josef looked hard at the medal and slipped it into his tunic pocket.

"But it's Christmas Day. Let's make the best of it. I am heading out on a round of company headquarters. I've got some cigarettes to distribute. And I might as well drop off this crude bomb with our expert. Would you like to come along?"

"Yes. We'll have a good talk. Do I have time to write a short letter to Mother?"

"Of course. Give her my love. I will write later today."

Conrad took a pencil stub from the desk and wrote.

December 25, 1942

Dearest Mother:

Christmas Day and I am celebrating with Josef. I have been out on the steppe and have not received any letters, but Josef tells me you are well and got the letter I sent out with Erich.

I don't know what to tell you now. Things have not worked out as we hoped. The time on the steppe was quite hard, but I have come home now. Whatever the future holds, Josef and I will face it together.

I don't know how much mail is getting

through, but Josef is a mighty Oberst now, and rank must have its privileges!

Be certain that whatever happens here, we shall come home one day. I think back fondly on our Christmases at home when Father was alive. How I used to love being led through to the magical parlor where the tree sparkled, loaded with candy, fruit and candles.

Do you remember how, on St. Nicholas's night, Father used to make us put a shoe on the hearth to be filled with treats if we had been good, or twigs if we had been bad?

I doubt if Josef's and my dinner today will rival the magnificent geese of the past or your famous fruit bread and spice bars, but at least we will be able to sing the old carols with fervor. We shall do our best to make this a true German Christmas and toast your health and Father's memory.

I feel very close to you now.

Josef sends his love and says he will write later today.

Happy Christmas and all my love.
Conrad

"I've left the back of the page blank for your letter," Conrad said.

"Thanks. I'll write it when we have done the rounds."

Conrad wrapped the letter around his pencil and stuffed it into his tunic pocket. Then he struggled into his jacket and boots.

The brothers crawled out of the bunker into the open air. It was bitterly cold and a stiff wind was blowing snow over the rubble, but after sleep and some food, it seemed much less harsh to Conrad than yesterday, and the thin covering of snow obscured some of the destruction and squalor.

The first thing Conrad noticed was the grand piano. It was sitting in what must have been the parlor of an important Communist official's house. The house was gone, but the piano had survived to sit majestically amid the ruins, its once-gleaming finish scored and chipped by numerous bullets and shell fragments. The missing lid exposed a nest of broken, twisted strings. Such a thing amid the rubble was so bizarre that Conrad stopped to stare.

"Do you want to play a tune?" Josef asked. "You should have been here the day the shrapnel shell exploded and the fragments cut the strings. It was like the devil playing that Wagner thing you like so much."

"*Götterdämmerung*?"

"Yes, that's it. The Twilight of the Gods. Didn't the heroine throw herself on her lover's funeral pyre at the end?"

"Brunnhilde. Yes, she did."

"I sometimes wonder," Josef said, gazing at the ruined piano. "Is the Sixth Army the Führer's Brunnhilde, throwing ourselves on his funeral pyre?"

Five months earlier, Conrad would have been shocked at Josef's words and denied them vehemently. Victory had been assured as he had ridden over the steppe in Lili. Now Lili was destroyed and her crew dead. Perhaps it was the end of the world.

"But the cold weather will keep the Ivans quiet," Josef said, breaking into his brother's thoughts, "and we can at least pretend we are having a proper Christmas.

"Now." Josef balanced the sack of grenades on his hip. "Follow me and do exactly what I do. Thankfully, C Company's not too far."

Ducking low, Josef set off behind a ruined wall. Conrad felt ridiculously happy. This was the worst place on earth. The best they could hope for was capture and prison camp. They would probably never see home or Mother again, yet Conrad felt content: he and Josef were together.

"I'm glad I found you," he said.

Josef half turned to look at Conrad. His red hair provided one of the few patches of color in the monochromatic world. "I'm glad you did too, little brother," he said with a smile. Turning back, Josef stood up a little straighter, exposing his head for a moment in a shell hole in the wall.

Conrad never heard the shot. Josef's head suddenly snapped back and he slumped to the ground.

Instinctively, Conrad looked to his right. Through the shell hole, he had the briefest glimpse of a figure in a window of a ruined building some distance away before bullets began to chip the wall around him. Conrad dropped and examined his brother.

The bullet had entered above Josef's left eye, traveled downward and exited through a gaping tear below his left ear. Josef had died instantly.

Realization that he was alone again came slowly to Conrad. He felt overwhelming rage — at Josef, at the war, at the Russian who had fired the shot. He fumbled for the medal in Josef's pocket, pulled it out and pinned it at his throat.

"I'll earn it, Josef," he said. "I'll make you and Father proud."

The firing had stopped, and Conrad risked a glimpse at the window. Empty. It must have been a sniper, firing from the ruined third floor of the building across the square.

Conrad lifted the sack and half-crawled, half-walked to the end of the wall. Lying there he had a clear view of the square without exposing more than one eye. He waited. The cold seeped through his clothing and the wind made his eyes sting, but the hatred inside was colder. There was nothing left to live for. Josef and all his friends were dead. Even if he survived this battle, Conrad would never make it home again. All the arrogant dreams and childish ideas that had filled his head so many months before had vanished. This was the end of the world — *Götterdämmerung*. The only thing left was to avenge Josef, even though Conrad understood that his revenge was pointless, that it simply added to the horror and would do no good.

Through the swirling snow, Conrad saw a movement. It was no more than a shadow, but it was enough. Dragging the sack behind him, he worked his way around the open square. He didn't care about hiding, he was in a hurry.

On the far side, he lay down and waited. His feet and fingers were numb and his cheeks felt as if they were being bombarded with needles. Conrad just stuffed his right hand into his left armpit to keep the fingers warm enough to pull the pin out of one of the grenades.

He ignored the numbness creeping up his legs. He welcomed the concealing snow that was beginning to lie on his back. He was becoming part of the ruined landscape. A rat scuttled up to investigate his face but left when it discovered he was still breathing.

Two figures dressed in white camouflage suits emerged from the rubble to his right, crouching low. Conrad lay still — just another snow-covered body among many.

Eventually, the two figures moved. Using the cover well, they passed within five meters of Conrad and disappeared down a hole in the building in front of him.

Breaking into a stumbling run on his frozen legs, Conrad lurched forward, clutching the sack of explosives to his chest.

The bullet entered his side between his third and fourth rib. Traveling downward, it exploded against his fifth vertebra, shattering the bone and severing his spinal cord. Conrad felt no pain, only a sensation of having been kicked hard in the back. His legs folded and he collapsed forward onto the snow, the sack in front of him. His vision was filled with exploding stars, and he was having trouble breathing. An unpleasant bubbling sound was coming from somewhere deep inside.

Conrad grasped the pin of the grenade at the top of the sack and pulled. With the last of his strength, he pushed the sack over the lip of the hole into the blackness. It bumped and slithered out of sight.

The earth heaved and a blast of hot air and dust shot out of the hole. With a hollow rumbling sound, something big shifted underground. But Conrad knew nothing.

SERGEI

Sergei can feel the rifle digging into his side as he lies behind the pile of bricks. It is awkward and much too large for him, but it makes him feel important, like a sniper. Sergei has carried it on all his foraging expeditions. He has learned how it works from soldiers and from practicing with the bolt, but he has only fired it once, at a rusted tin can. He missed and now has only two bullets left.

He slowly raises his head and peers over the bricks. Across the square is the house with the ruined piano. Something catches his eye, a flash of color in a gray world. Two Fascist officers have come up from a bunker. One has a shock of red hair. Sergei's mind races back to the German soldiers who rescued him from the fallen wall — they were led by a redheaded officer. Sergei stares, but the two men have disappeared behind a wall. Perhaps he will get another glimpse farther along. Yes, there is a hole in the wall. Sergei sees a flicker of red. The head snaps to one side as a single shot rings out, followed by a burst of machine-gun fire.

Sergei ducks back, confused. There's a sniper around; but the redheaded officer might be the one who saved his life.

Sergei peers over to where he heard the shot, the excitement at possibly seeing one of his sniper heroes chases away any sadness at one more death among so many.

Eventually, he is rewarded with the sight of two figures off to his left. They are moving carefully, using the cover well, and they are snipers. They are dressed in white camouflage suits. He can even see the scope on the rifle one carries. He wishes there was a scope on his rifle — then he wouldn't miss, and mad Tolstoy would stop demanding payment of a dead German soldier for his turnip.

As Sergei watches the two figures move through the rubble, the one with the scoped rifle glances in his direction. Sergei's heart leaps — it is Pavlova. He wants to jump up and wave, but he lies still — like a real sniper.

With a final look around, Pavlova and her companion disappear into a hole in the ruins. Suddenly, a ragged German soldier, clutching a sack, rises from a pile of frozen corpses and stumbles toward the hole. He is following Pavlova and her companion. Sergei will save her. Hauling his rifle up, he points it at the man. He doesn't aim properly, even closes his eyes as he squeezes the trigger, but the man is only a few meters away.

The rifle kicks back painfully into Sergei's shoulder and the crash almost deafens him. When he opens his eyes, the soldier is lying flat on the ground beside the hole.

Pavlova is safe — Sergei has saved her. He feels a surge of pride. Then he looks more closely. The man is not dead; he is fiddling with the bag in front of him and pushing it toward the hole. The soldier is just a boy. He doesn't look like the evil creatures Tolstoy is always talking about. The boy looks little different from hundreds of young Russian soldiers Sergei has seen.

He pushes the thought down. The boy is the enemy. He deserves to die.

With the last of his strength, the soldier pushes the sack down into the dark hole. Sergei feels rather than hears a deep rumbling and his pile of bricks moves ominously. A cloud of dirty smoke and dust shoots out of the hole.

Sergei's frightened, but fascinated too. When the dust clears, the mouth of the hole is closed. Sergei knows Pavlova will be working her way toward some other exit to kill more Fascists.

The soldier Sergei has shot is lying still now. After a long time, Sergei's curiosity gets the better of him and he crawls forward to investigate the body. Dead Germans rarely offer good pickings these days, but there is always the possibility of some sausage or cigarettes that can be traded.

A large patch of dark blood has formed around the long tear in the back of the soldier's uniform. Sergei shudders. He has seen plenty of blood and bullet holes, but none that he has caused. Screwing up his courage, he rolls the body over. It is still warm. There is a glint of metal at the man's throat. An Iron Cross — soldiers give bread for one of these. And he can show it to Tolstoy to prove he has paid for the turnip.

A quick search reveals little else of value: a pencil stub — that might come in useful. He throws away the scrap paper with its illegible scrawl — he can't read German.

"Sergei," his mother's voice echoes through the cold air. "Where are you? Come home, you'll get into trouble."

VASILY

"I love you."

Yelena stood in front of Vasily, smiling, in a blue sequined ball gown. Her hair was piled on top of her head, jewelry glinted at her ears and throat and her skin glowed with health and life. Vasily was the happiest man in the world.

Raucous laughter tore through Vasily's dream. Yelena faded as he struggled to pull himself back into reality. A sinking feeling replaced his euphoria. Had he spoken out loud? Would he open his eyes to see the other soldiers in the bunker gathered around to make fun of him?

Reluctantly, Vasily dragged his eyelids up. No soldiers leered down at him. The laughter had been at some crude joke across the room. Only Yelena's face, much dirtier than in the dream but wearing the same smile, gazed at him in the pale yellow light of an oil lantern.

"Here," she said, handing Vasily a piece of sausage and a hunk of bread. "Eat breakfast. We have work to do."

Vasily hauled himself to a sitting position and took a mouthful of the sausage. It was dry and difficult to chew, but it tasted spicy and good. Working on the sausage distracted Vasily from the worry that he might have spoken his dream words out loud. They were true, but he couldn't say them to Yelena. Even after they had worked together for months, her confidence made him feel weak and insignificant.

They were like an old married couple, Vasily thought wryly. They lived their own life separate from the vulgar soldiers who shared the cellar: they knew each other and each relied on the other to get by.

Could their special relationship exist if they were not killing Fascists? The idea of a normal life with Yelena in some Moscow apartment or Urals farm was too foreign to conceive of. Besides, if he began to envisage a future for them after this war, he wouldn't be able to work efficiently. His priority would be making sure Yelena was safe, not helping her kill the enemy — and that would be dangerous for both of them. Vasily had to suppress his feelings, but he couldn't control his dreams.

"Stop daydreaming and let's go," Yelena ordered. Grabbing his submachine gun and spare magazines, Vasily followed her across the cellar. Soldiers looked up disinterestedly as they passed. The population of the cellar had turned over three or four times since he and Yelena had established themselves in their corner.

Certainly, he recognized none of the faces that turned toward him. Only Nikolai remained, drinking too much rough vodka, but alive. Instinctively, Vasily felt his pocket for the cartridge lighter Nikolai had given him on that drunken evening a month ago. He found himself flicking it in moments of stress, just as he had seen Nikolai do so often.

Pushing through the heavy curtain that covered the cellar doorway and prevented any light escaping, Yelena and Vasily climbed the rubble-strewn steps. At the surface, they huddled behind a broken stretch of wall and let their eyes become accustomed to the predawn darkness. This was the most dangerous part of their day, the only time Yelena was forced into a routine — and all routines were potentially deadly. A German sniper might have spotted something from one of the taller ruins across the square and be waiting for the slightest movement to give him a target. It was less likely on a cloudy morning like this when the moon was obscured and snow swirled around, but Vasily knew that Yelena would not relax her precautions.

For what seemed like an age, the pair sat motionless as fingers of cold searched for a break in their clothing. It was at least twenty degrees below zero and Vasily was grateful for his padded suit. They were normally only issued to snipers, but Yelena had managed to get one for him too.

Very slowly, Vasily scanned his surroundings. The skeletal shapes of buildings were forming against the sky. To the north, dull explosions and the pop of small-arms fire indicated a struggle for some pile of rubble, and flames reflected a dull red off the low snow clouds.

Satisfied that they were not being hunted, Yelena tapped Vasily on the arm and moved off. Slowly and silently, the pair worked their way around the edge of the square. Because they traveled through the ruined buildings rather than on the relatively open streets, their journey was slow. It was an hour before they passed the scattered sounds of fighting at the Red October Factory.

The fighting at Red October had been some of the fiercest, and thousands of Russian bodies covered the land around the factory. Since Vasily and Yelena had fought there, the Germans had taken it and turned it into a fortress, but this was a good sign: they were on the defensive, digging in and holding on rather than attacking.

Outside the city, the German relief offensive had been stopped fifty kilometers away, and the increasing number of prisoners were telling of reduced rations, shortages of ammunition and fuel, and deaths from frostbite and malnutrition.

Now that the weather had turned bitterly cold, the Volga had frozen solid. This and a German shortage of shells allowed a regular flow of supplies to Rodimtsev's 13th Guards. Everyone had high spirits. Even Chuikov, the stern commander of the Stalingrad battle, had crossed the river for the first time since September (although rumor had it he had got so drunk that he had fallen through the ice on the way back and had to be unceremoniously fished out).

No one now doubted that the battle of Stalingrad would be a great Russian victory. What was important was to make it a crushing victory. To everyone's surprise, the German Sixth Army had made no attempt to break out and link up with the relief attack. Certainly, Hitler had said that the German army would never surrender Stalingrad, but surely that was just rhetoric. Holding on in the ruins simply doomed hundreds of thousands of men to death or captivity — it made no military sense.

But Red October was not Yelena's destination. For two days, she and Vasily had been scouting an area between the factory and Mamaev Kurgan. Yelena thought there was a command bunker in the area and she was now focusing on finally killing a German officer.

"I can't kill every Fascist soldier," she had said, "but I can behead the monster. For every officer I kill, there is a squad or a tank crew that are leaderless and less effective." Despite an impressive toll of kills, rank higher than sergeant eluded her. The hunt for an officer was becoming an obsession; hence, the long journeys before dawn and the long days watching.

She had chosen the day carefully. Although the old Russian Christmas was still thirteen days away, the Germans had been heard celebrating the night before. Perhaps they would let their guard down today.

The pair had spent the previous day lying motionless and frozen, watching the movements of German soldiers around a hole that Yelena was sure was an entrance to a bunker. She had had many opportunities to kill signalers, runners or ordinary soldiers; but she had held her fire. It was an officer she wanted.

The site she had chosen for their deadly vigil was the third floor of a large department store. Soldiers lived in the store's cavernous basement, and the main floor had been fought over so many times that it was littered with bodies of both sides. But the upper two floors were deserted. They had been bombed and shelled until only a skeletal framework remained.

Dawn was painting the eastern horizon by the time Vasily and Yelena edged through the ruins. Naked display mannequins lay everywhere, mimicking the carnage outside. The roof was gone, opening the floor to the sky, and only the wall closest to the enemy retained any shape. The pair wormed their way past fallen beams, piles of bricks and jagged holes that gaped to the floor below.

Eventually, they reached the places Yelena had chosen. She crouched beside what used to be a window close to the corner of the floor. Vasily lay at a shell hole two meters away. The view was the same as anywhere else in Stalingrad, a wasteland of broken walls and rubble. The landscape appeared empty, and a newcomer would find it hard to believe that thousands of men were fighting desperately all around. When they were not attacking or moving position, both sides spent most of their time underground living in basements and traveling, where possible, through sewers and tunnels.

Vasily removed his helmet and pulled the hood of his suit up to cover his hair. He settled himself as comfortably as possible with his machine gun in front of him and fixed his eyes on the pile of rubble that Yelena thought concealed the entrance to the command post. Vasily located it by the wrecked grand piano in the ruins of the house beside it. It made him think of his father's old upright piano and the evenings of singing around it. What magnificent sounds would a grand piano make? But this piano would never make music again.

Vasily settled himself as comfortably as he could — it might be a long day. His job was to provide distracting fire if Yelena wanted it, scout in unfamiliar terrain and protect her if they were attacked. He doubted if any of those roles would be needed today. His and Yelena's work had become almost routine — a far cry from the first chaotic weeks after their nightmare journey across the river.

Vasily watched a soldier crawl out from behind the pile of rubble and dart behind a ruined wall. It was an easy shot, even for Vasily. Perhaps he would volunteer for sniper school. Some of the most famous snipers, like Zaitsev, were said to have been withdrawn from the fight in order to teach at the school. But Vasily knew it would never happen. He was a good shot, and with training he might make the grade, but he was missing two vital elements of the successful sniper — cold-bloodedness and patience.

Vasily had no problem killing Fascists. He could toss a grenade into a crowded room or mow down waves of attackers in the heat of battle, but a sniper, in that moment before pulling the trigger, had to look his unknowing victim in the face. It was too personal. And the victim often seemed so mundane. Vasily had seen Yelena kill men who were eating breakfast, shaving or attending to a call of nature.

Also, in order to concentrate for hours at a time, a sniper had to be able to detach from mind and body. Vasily couldn't do that. He was always being distracted by an annoying itch somewhere or by daydreams. Increasingly, the daydreams were about Yelena.

Vasily's mind drifted back to last night's dream. Yelena had been beautiful and they had been safe. He didn't know where — it looked like Moscow but it felt like somewhere much farther east. The overwhelming thing was safety. Vasily realized that he had not felt safe for a single moment in the past three months. What was it like? He couldn't remember. The feeling of safety was buried so deep that it surfaced only in his dreams. When he was awake his survival depended on the awareness that came from not feeling safe.

"Did you ever celebrate Christmas?" Yelena's voice reached Vasily through his daydream. He glanced over at his partner. She was frozen in position, and her gaze was fixed on the scope of her rifle, but she was talking out of the side of her mouth.

"No," Vasily replied. "It's just the priests' way of distracting workers and the poor from their revolutionary duty with baubles and mumbo jumbo." It was the proper thing to say, what he had been taught; but even as the words came out, they sounded hollow.

Vasily frowned. Doubt was disconcerting; it was much easier to believe.

"When I was a child back in the twenties," Yelena went on, "we used to eat a special meal on Christmas Eve. It was never called 'Holy Supper' as in the old days, but it was still special. We weren't allowed to eat all day. When it began to get dark, I was sent outside to watch for the first star. That was the signal that we could all sit down at the table.

"The meal was always the same, no meat but twelve different kinds of food. My favorite was *kutya*. It was a porridge made from wheat berries for hope, grain for immortality, honey for happiness and poppy seeds for success and untroubled rest. It was eaten from a common dish in the middle of the table to symbolize the unity of the family. My father always threw the first spoonful at the ceiling. If it stuck, we would have a good year.

"The old people told how, after Holy Supper, everyone used to walk from house to house singing carols. Of course *we* had to celebrate indoors."

Yelena's gaze remained fixed, but her tone had become wistful. Vasily didn't know what to say. He had heard that in some remote areas, the old ways had gone on long after the revolution. He had always supposed it had only been among illiterate peasants who knew no better. Yelena talking about banned activity with such nostalgia was a shock.

"Mother always put lots of honey in the *kutya* to make it good and sticky," Yelena went on. "The only year it didn't stick to the ceiling was the year Father was taken away."

Vasily stared at Yelena's profile. She had made throwing porridge at the ceiling an act of rebellion, and in doing so she had made the system being rebelled against look stupid.

"A waste of good porridge," Vasily said.

"Perhaps," Yelena conceded, "but superstition is powerful. And at least we didn't believe stories about clever farmers outwitting talking bears in the forest."

Vasily chuckled at the gibe. "Just because you've never heard a bear talk doesn't mean —"

"Shh!" cut through Vasily's sentence like a knife. Yelena had seen something. There! A movement at the corner of a wall beside the bunker entrance.

"Do you see it?" Yelena whispered.

"Yes."

"It's an officer. Maybe two. He is leaving the bunker, so he will have to pass that shell hole in the wall to his right. If he doesn't duck low enough, I'll get him. I won't have time for two shots. As soon as I shoot, you fire off your entire magazine. If there is a second one he might do something dumb."

Vasily aimed at the window opening and curled his finger around the trigger. He tried to keep himself as still as Yelena, but his senses were so heightened by the tension that each tiny lump of dirt on the floor felt like a mountain digging into him.

Time dragged: perhaps the officer had taken a different route, or maybe he crawled on his stomach below the hole. That's what Vasily would do. Yelena had taught him never to pass a window or shell hole that faced the enemy. Nine times out of ten nothing would happen, but that tenth time, you were dead. Was this the tenth time for the German officer?

Then the officer was there, his head looking ridiculously big and his red hair too bright. For what seemed like an age he was framed in the jagged hole. Yelena's rifle coughed, the head snapped back and the man dropped from sight.

Vasily had a glimpse of the second man's face before he squeezed the trigger and held it down until the magazine was empty.

"My officer!" Yelena said triumphantly, sliding away from her position. "A high-ranking one too. Maybe we got both of them."

Yelena was smiling broadly at Vasily. "Come on. Let's go back and celebrate. Maybe we can even find some porridge."

Vasily awoke in a darkness deeper than any he could have imagined. Only the irritating dust told him his eyes were open. Was he blind? His ears were filled with a mighty roaring sound that seemed to come from within his head. He reached up — his ears were wet and sticky.

Vasily remembered unrelated images — snow falling softly, bullets picking out puffs of brick dust around a hole in a wall, an explosion hurling him into blackness, Yelena's smile.

Yelena! Where was she? He called quietly into the darkness. Even if there had been a reply, he would not have heard it over the roaring in his head. Then he remembered Nikolai's lighter. Fumbling in his pocket, Vasily pulled it out and spun the wheel with his finger. On the third attempt, the wick caught and a pale bluish light suffused the area. The first thing he saw was the top of Yelena's head lying by his foot. Terrified, he leaned forward to touch her. Rough bone ends grated together in his hips and a wave of sickening pain surged through him before he blacked out.

Vasily came to, the lighter still in his hand. He spun the wheel again. The pain in his hip had subsided to a dull ache; he suspected that his pelvis was broken. Holding the lighter as high as he could, Vasily took stock of his surroundings.

He was lying in the corner of the cellar he and Yelena had been passing through when the explosion came. The collapsed roof completely blocked the way they had entered, and there seemed no way through in the direction they had been going.

Yelena lay on her left side, her head level with Vasily's right ankle. Her legs were buried under the collapsed roof and her body was twisted at an awkward angle. Vasily forced down his rising panic.

"Yelena!" he yelled. It sounded hollow inside his head, as if coming from a long way away. It produced no response.

Vasily looked around for something he could use to reach out to her. Her precious rifle lay beside him, the scope bent out of shape, the butt under her shoulder. Transferring the lighter to his left hand, Vasily pulled the barrel of the rifle toward him.

To his immense relief, he saw Yelena move. With an obvious effort, she twisted her neck to look at him. She grimaced in pain, but her eyes were bright and focused. Her lips moved, but no sound made it through the roaring in Vasily's head.

He touched each of his ears experimentally. The wetness around his right one shone red in the flame of the lighter, but his left ear didn't seem too bad. Twisting his head as far as he could, he strained to make out what Yelena was saying. The words came through as if shouted by someone far away.

"My back," he heard. "Broken."

"My pelvis too, I think."

For a long moment, the pair looked at each other in silence. The flickering lighter flame threw weird, dancing shadows on the walls and reflected off the thick dust in the air. The muscles in Yelena's neck tensed as she fought a wave of pain.

"There's no way out?" she asked eventually.

"No. A shell must have exploded in the entrance."

"Not a shell. I heard something roll down the slope before the explosion."

"We're not going to get out, are we?"

The realization flooded over Vasily. Neither of them could move and no one, except an enemy, knew where they were. Even if they were dug out, they would probably not survive the treatment that could be given amid the ruins. All they could look forward to was increasing cold, darkness and pain. Death would be welcome. As if in response to Vasily's thoughts, the lighter flame flickered and the darkness moved closer.

"Vasily." Yelena's voice brought him back from his morbid thoughts. "I don't think I can stand the pain much longer."

"I'm sorry," Vasily said.

"Can you help me?"

He felt tears sting his eyes. "I would do anything if I could."

With immense effort, Yelena reached her right arm over her head and pushed her rifle against Vasily's leg.

"No!" he shouted in horror as he realized what she wanted.

Yelena convulsed in pain and a trickle of blood seeped out at the corner of her mouth. She looked up at him pleadingly.

"I can't."

"You must." Yelena's gaze never left him. "You have helped me in everything, Assistant Sniper Vasily Sarayev. Help me in this one last thing."

Yelena gasped as another wave of pain overcame her.

That decided it. Hauling the rifle savagely toward him, Vasily turned it around and pointed the barrel at Yelena's head. Using only his right hand, he couldn't keep the barrel steady. To use both hands, he would have to put the lighter down. How could he aim in the darkness.

As if she understood, Yelena reached back and held the barrel steady against her head. "Thank you."

"I love you," Vasily said, and pulled the trigger.

THE END

Saturday, December 25, 2004

S E R G E I

Sergei Andropov's arthritic joints hurt. The cold has seeped into his old bones. How long has he been sitting with all these ancient memories? It was all so long ago — the ruins, the bombing, the redheaded officer and the price Sergei paid for Tolstoy's turnip. But there's something on the edge of Sergei's awareness that is nagging at him to remember. Something that will make sense of it all.

Sergei swings the flashlight beam over the decayed corpses. It is then he notices the scrap of paper on the sitting body's lap. It is a letter. Screwing up his tired eyes, Sergei reads.

> Father:
>
> I do not know how much I will be able to write.
>
> We have won this great battle and now, I think, we will win this war. It will be a great celebration, but

I am not coming home.

I have done wonderful things, and terrible things. I have seen men commit horrors that were unimaginable only a few months ago, and I have fallen in love. I wish you could have met her. Her name was Yelena Pavlova and I have just killed her. I will die soon too, but for a moment in this madness I was happy.

My lighter is running out and the darkness presses in. I must stop.

Your loving son

Assistant Sniper Vasily Sarayev

Sergei wipes the tears from his cheeks. They hadn't escaped, the two figures he had watched on this day, all those years ago. His sniper hero had died while he had rummaged through the uniform of the soldier who had killed her.

Gently, Sergei folds the fragile paper and tucks it into the tatters of Vasily's uniform. Sighing heavily, he clambers up into the harsh glare of the arc light. It is time to go home — before he gets into trouble.

AFTERWORD

The last frozen and starving remnants of Field Marshall von Paulus's Sixth Army finally surrendered on February 2, 1943 (day 229 since the beginning of this story). The dead were burned in piles on the open steppe and the survivors marched off to a captivity from which few returned.

Stalingrad was horrific for a number of reasons. As Gottfried points out, sending tanks to fight in ruined cities makes no sense. However, Hitler was obsessed with taking the city and Stalin with holding it. Both men ordered their troops to fight for every room of every house. They were never to take one step backward. This robbed officers of any tactical or strategic flexibility and condemned soldiers to a pointless, bloody battle of attrition. The egos of these two madmen cost millions of lives.

Stalingrad — Volgograd, as it is now known — has been rebuilt. A vast memorial on Mamaev Kurgan commemorates the dead, whose bodies are still being uncovered today.

ACKNOWLEDGMENTS

Antony Beevor's *Stalingrad: The Fateful Siege, 1942–1943* provided much of the historical background for this tale. A visual sense of the battle was gleaned from the remarkable images collected in Stephen Walsh's *Stalingrad* and from the movie *Enemy at the Gates*. The emotional struggles of the soldiers were found in Theodor Plievier's novel *Stalingrad*, which is based on interviews with survivors. Web searches provided details such as the layout and dimensions of a Panzer Mark IV and the number of rounds in the magazine of Vasily's weapon.

Unlike the commanders of the armies at Stalingrad, Charis Wahl has once more shown flexibility and creativity in helping turn this into the story it is.